WILD GOLD

Heggerty was bushwhacked by gunslingers and left to seek survival in the searing desert. He finally made it to the town of Bliss, where a mysterious marshal told Heggerty of a vanished shipment of gold and the unavenged death of his son. The last thing he'd reckoned on was a trek through sacred Apache country with the enigmatic marshal in a desperate bid to recover the gold. He then had to come to grips with the gunslingers and face a showdown with the woman who had bull-whipped him to within an inch of his life...

WILD GOLD

WILD GOLD

by
Jack Reason

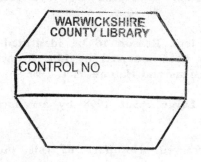
Dales Large Print Books
Long Preston, North Yorkshire,
England.

British Library Cataloguing in Publication Data.

Reason, Jack
  Wild gold.

A catalogue record for this book is
available from the British Library

ISBN 1-85389-798-1 pbk

First published in Great Britain by Robert Hale Ltd., 1996

Published in Large Print 1998 by arrangement with Robert
Hale Ltd.

Dales Large Print is an imprint of
Library Magna Books Ltd.
Printed and bound in Great Britain by
T.J. International Ltd., Cornwall, PL28 8RW.

For R.B.
and the prospect of many
more conversations

ONE

Charlie Maggs rocked rythmically to and fro in his chair on the veranda of the homestead a mile short of Bliss and squinted into the heat-haze without blinking. He was laying even odds with himself that the man crossing the desert on foot would make it to the shade within the hour. Make it, or drop where he was and fry.

Charlie had been watching the man since he first appeared as a shimmering blur on the horizon. A tall, firm-shouldered figure; steady steps, even pace, never faltering. Determined, maybe angry, a man with a heap of fretting on his mind—and sure as hell a mite thirsty by now.

He wondered where and when he had lost his mount? Whisper Pass, Muddy Creek? Either way, he had walked a fair distance since sun-up. Maybe he had come

9

out of the mountains, slipped an Apache ambush. Lucky for him if he had. Maybe he had been bush-whacked by roughriders.

Charlie Maggs spat into the sand and listened to the spittle sizzle. It was hot, too darned hot for an old man to move; too hot for walking, save when your life depended on it. He hummed to the creak of the chair, blinked his tired eyes and focused again on the man. Still coming on, same pace, same angry stride. Yep, he reckoned, fella was going to make it...

Heggerty spat, dust and sand. The sweat in his neck, across his shoulders, seeping in steady trickles down his back to his waist and on to his thighs and legs, was warm and sticky. His eyes were narrowed and aching beneath the brim of his hat; his face wet and grimy, his lips already beginning to crack like parchment, and his throat—his goddamn throat—felt like wood chippings mixed with ash. He tried hard not to swallow, and concentrated his legs, through even strides, the firm footfalls, just straight on... Into the furnace of the sun.

'Sonofabitch!' he croaked, and clenched his fingers to spongy fists that oozed sweat instantly. His lips tightened, his anger boiled as he recalled for the hundredth time the events of two nights back...

He had reached the shade of the cottonwoods in the late afternoon of that day, glad of the chance to rest up after a long ride. He had tended to the Appaloosa mare, settled her, and by dusk lit a fire, made coffee, cooked a meal and finally leaned back on his bedroll to savour the cooling drift of the evening breeze.

Life was feeling good. He had passed quietly through the tumbledown town of Sandrocks, pausing only briefly to stock up with fresh provisions, and headed south-west on the trail for Whisper Pass. From there, he would cross the desert, reach Bliss and have himself a few days' rest, then on again, deep into the southern territories. Good going, he had reflected as the night closed in. Whisper Pass in the morning, Bliss the following day... A shave, a bath, drinks in the saloon, a game of poker, maybe a woman...

He had not been completely aware of slipping into the doze that would prelude sleep. He could remember the mare's gentle snort, her soft pawing, the murmur of the breeze in the cottonwoods, the gathering gloom, a sprinkling of high stars...

Had the mare's startled whinny come before the flash of light that scorched his eyes; had he imagined the images of the dark men before the thudding pain in his head, or had both been some twist of dreams into nightmare? The reality had been plain enough when he came to in the faintest slip of first light—the mare, his provisions, his bedroll, everything, had gone. What he had was what he stood in, plus, thankfully, his still holstered and belted twin Colts.

Bushwhacked!

It had taken him nearly an hour to clear his head and begin to think straight. There had been four riders—that much he could figure from the boot and hoof marks—and they had headed fast for Whisper Pass.

Biggest loss was the mare; the most critical the fact that the raiders had taken his water.

Whisper Pass had proved the salvation on that count when he finally reached it later that morning. The trickle of bedrock stream had not dried up and he was able to satisfy his thirst to the full. But then came the prospect of the desert. He had no choice but to make for Bliss. Sandrocks was too far back and mostly through Apache country. No place for a man on foot. Nothing for it. He would have to face the desert.

Heggerty had been walking since an hour before sun-up, his pace steady, his concentration fixed on the clear tracks left in the sand by the riders as they headed for Bliss. No mistaking the mare's prints; no mistaking the speed of the riders. They were in a hurry, and so was Heggerty. There was a score to be settled, and with luck he would be in Bliss to pay out in full.

But now, in the high heat and glare of noon, the effort of walking was taking its

13

toll. Heggerty's steps and the pace he had set himself had not faltered, but the ache in his muscles had deepened; his sight too had blurred to a floating mist of vague images through which the far horizon drifted like a receding tide.

Even so, Heggerty had not failed to identify the shape of the homestead. That was no mirage, no twist of the imagination. That was a roof, a chimney, the stark outline of corral fencing, and there were shadows, black as crows on the sprawl of sand. Maybe there was somebody there. Maybe they would see him.

In another hour, Heggerty had come to within a quarter-mile of the homestead, but his stride had shortened, his steps were heavier, his legs weaker, and his arms hung loose and lifeless at his sides. He stumbled, halted, came on again. He tried to call out, but no sounds came from his parched throat. He blinked tightly, felt the sting of sweat in his eyes. Moving again...step by careful step...closer, until he could see the homestead's windows, its door, a veranda. There had to be somebody...

He never felt a thing when he thudded to the ground and lay perfectly still in the searing sand.

'Don't move too soon,' said a distant voice. 'Just take it easy. Here, sip slowly.'

Heggerty felt the cool touch of water at his lips. He swallowed, blinked, opened his eyes. The face above him belonged to a girl; young, blue-eyed, snub-nosed, full, delicate mouth, bright corn-coloured hair tied back in a pony-tail. Loose working shirt and tight pants. There was a smudge of dirt on her right cheek.

She smiled cheerfully. 'How yuh feelin'?'

Heggerty blinked again and propped himself up on an elbow. Where was he? The homestead; a neat, orderly room, table, chairs, a cooking range, drapes at the window, still, flat shadows. 'Rough—but thanks,' he croaked, and ran a hand over his face. 'Where am I?'

'Charlie Magg's place,' smiled the girl. 'He's my uncle. I'm Joni. Pleased t' meet yuh.'

'Name's Heggerty.'

15

'Stranger hereabouts? Uncle Charlie said as how yuh were. He saw yuh comin'. Trouble is, his old legs don't let him get about none too good these days. I was in town with Tentrees—he's our Apache hand—so Uncle couldn't do a deal f' yuh till yuh got close. Watchin' yuh all mornin' he was. Reckoned yuh'd make it, though. He was tryin' t' drag yuh int' the shade when I got back.' The girl offered him another mug of water. 'Sip at it,' she said.

Heggerty winced and sat up.

'What happened?' asked the girl. 'Yuh get bush-whacked?'

'Yeah...bush-whacked,' said Heggerty as he began to tell her of the events of the night in the cottonwoods.

'Yuh reckon four riders?' said Joni. 'That figures.'

'Yuh see them?' asked Heggerty.

'Talk in town this mornin' was that four men rode in a day back. Roughriders. I didn't see them, but I saw yuh Appaloosa. She's at Joe Pine's livery.'

Heggerty's eyes narrowed, his lips tightened as he came slowly to his feet. 'Be

16

obliged if I could wash up, miss, then I'll be—'

'Yuh ain't plannin' on going int' town now, are yuh? Yuh ain't fit, mister. Nothin' like it.'

'I'll manage,' murmured Heggerty.

The girl flounced round the table, lifting and moving things on it with angry determination. 'Darned fool crazy, if yuh ask me! Them riders ain't goin' no place, not yet awhile. Too busy in the saloon. Couple of hours ain't goin' to make much odds.'

'Yuh probably right, miss, but I don't see it like that.'

''Course yuh don't,' said Charlie Maggs, hobbling into the room with the aid of a stick. 'Seen that in yuh soon as I clapped eyes on yuh.' His toothless smile broadened beneath grey twinkling eyes. 'Said t' m'self, now there's a fella who keeps goin', come what may. Once he's got his sights on somethin', that's it. No shiftin' him. That's what I said.'

'Obliged t' yuh for what yuh did, Mister Maggs. Guess yuh saved m' life.'

The old man slapped his lips together. 'Don't know about that, son. It was Joni here and Tentrees who got yuh inside.' He took a step forward and stared intently into Heggerty's face. 'Tell yuh what, though, mister, I seen them riders Joni's been tellin' yuh about. Passed west of here. I seen 'em plain enough, and yuh mark it they ain't here f' no rest. Nossir! they're here f' a purpose. Somebody's hired 'em. Somebody right here in Bliss is plannin' somethin' that calls f' gunslingers. And I reckon I ain't wrong.' He grinned. 'Best saddle up the bay f' the man, Joni.'

The girl flashed Heggerty an anxious glance, and did not miss the sudden glint in his eyes.

TWO

Heggerty cantered the bay gently along the dust trail to Bliss. The afternoon sun was still high, the heat thick and haze-filled, but the sweat on his brow, in his neck and across his shoulders, was bearable. He was relaxed in spite of the still stinging sunburn of his desert ordeal, and content now in the thought that he knew where to find the Appaloosa mare and that she would be waiting for him.

He was less happy with Charlie Magg's theory concerning the four riders.

Roughriders and bushwhackers they were sure enough, but hired gunslingers brought to Bliss for a purpose? That was not so easy to accept. And yet—where had they come from that night in the cottonwoods, and why had they ridden so purposefully and hurriedly to Bliss? Why, come to that, were they still there?

The questions intrigued, but Heggerty reckoned they were Bliss's problem, not his. His concern was the mare.

Bliss was a surprisingly bustling, busy town with an air of prosperity about it. The buildings were neat, clean and active. There was a saloon—Twilight's—an hotel, a bank with an imposing facade, two or three stores, a carpenter's, saddlery and gunsmith's, and, at the far end of the main street, Joe Pine's livery.

Heggerty eased the bay to a walk as he approached the open frontage where a thick-shouldered man—Joe Pine, he guessed—was absorbed with a mound of tack.

'Howdy,' said Heggerty, reining up.

The man turned and squinted at Heggerty through the sun's glare. He grunted and went back to the tack. 'Yuh bringin' business, mister, or passin' through?'

'Lookin',' said Heggerty.

'Somethin' specific in mind?'

'Appaloosa mare.'

Pine eased a saddle to the ground with

all the careful slowness he could muster, paused a moment, and then turned again, this time shielding his eyes against the glare with a raised hand.

'Appaloosa, yuh say?' he said, a soft tremor in his voice.

'S'right,' said Heggerty, dismounting and leading the bay to the hitching rail. 'High-steppin', wild-eyed, soft-nosed, paws clean with her left hoof. No mistakin' her.'

'Ain't seen no Appaloosa,' began Pine.

'Come on, Joe, that ain't bein' quite honest, is it?' said Heggerty, moving towards the darkened enclosures of the livery.

Joe Pine reached for a loose wooden stake at his side, caught the sudden flash of Heggerty's glance, the gentle tap of his fingers on the butts of his Colts, and dropped the stake.

'Let's take a look, Joe,' said Heggerty.

Pine stepped ahead of Heggerty to bar his way. 'Yuh ain't got no right t' go nosin' in there, mister,' he growled. 'That's trespassin'.'

Heggerty hesitated. His eyes narrowed

and darkened. 'Yuh got an Appaloosa mare in there, Joe?'

'None of your business if I have.'

'It's stolen!' snapped Heggerty. 'The mare belongs t' me. Now, we goin' t' take a look in there peaceful like, or do I have t' deal with you first?'

There was the softest snort of a horse from inside the livery.

'That's her!' said Heggerty. 'Know that sound anywhere.'

A lather of sweat had broken out on Joe Pine's brow. 'OK, mister, so I got an Appaloosa mare. Four fellas brought her in day or so back. Said t' take care of her f' a while till they were ready t' leave.'

'Bushwhackers, mister! Bushwhackers!'

Pine frowned. 'How'd yuh know?'

''Cus I'm the one they bushwhacked!'

Heggerty brushed past Pine and strode into the livery. The mare's eyes flashed at him. She tossed her head, flicked her tail, pawed excitedly and snorted.

'OK, gal,' soothed Heggerty, patting the mount's neck. 'Steady now. Easy. Where the hell yuh been, eh?'

The mare snorted again.

'Nice-lookin' horse, mister,' said a voice at Heggerty's back.

Heggerty turned sharply, one hand already on the butt of a Colt, and peered into the gloom.

'Not much doubt who owns her,' said the voice again as the tall, tanned, well-dressed man stepped into the half light. His bright eyes narrowed on Heggerty's hold on the Colt. 'No need f' that, mister. I ain't spoilin' f' anythin'.'

Heggerty relaxed. 'I know yuh?' he asked.

'Don't reckon so. Name's Logan. Marshal Josh Logan.'

'Heggerty. Yuh say Marshal? Yuh sittin' on the tails of them scum bushwhackers by any chance?'

'Sort of.'

'What's that mean?'

Logan looked to where Joe Pine hovered in the sun glow, then at Heggerty. 'Care t' join me f' a drink at the hotel, Heggerty? I gotta story t' tell—and I fancy yuh might like t'hear it.'

The marshal's room at the hotel was cool behind its closed drapes. Logan placed a bottle of whiskey and two glasses on the table and gestured for Heggerty to pull up a chair.

'Yuh walk in after yuh lost the mare?' he asked when he and Heggerty were seated facing each other.

'Yuh mean yuh believe I *was* bush-whacked?' said Heggerty.

'I believe yuh. No doubtin' that mare's yours, and I gotta pretty shrewd idea of how she got here. Yuh care t' fill me in on the detail?'

Heggerty recounted the events of that night. How he had crossed the desert and finally arrived at Charlie Magg's homestead. 'His niece was in town this mornin' and saw the mare. That's why I'm here,' he concluded, then added thoughtfully, 'But Charlie don't reckon them critters are bush-whackers. He thinks they're gunfighters.'

'Interestin',' said Logan, finishing his drink and pouring another. He topped up Heggerty's glass and was silent for a moment. 'Charlie's right,' he began, watching Heggerty closely. 'They ain't bushwhackers—and they very definitely are gunslingers.' He paused, stared intently, and continued, 'Ben Slocum, he's the eldest of the four. Been shootin' his way int' and outa trouble f' most of his life. Surprised he's still livin'. Emmett Stone, self-styled leader of the pack, cool, calm, cruel, and fast. Yuh don't tangle with Stone, 'ceptin' on yuh own terms. Cy Bennett, he's Stone's number two, with one eye on the top job. He ain't no gentleman, specially where woman are concerned. And lastly, Billy 'Lucky' Dimond, the baby. He joined up with Stone after shootin' three men and a sheriff back Nevada way. He's loud, wild and gun crazy.'

'Yuh seem t' know them well enough,' said Heggerty.

'Should do. Been a thorn in my side f' as long as I been a marshal.'

'So how come yuh here in Bliss?'

The marshal smiled ruefully. 'Some weeks back I was out East. Routine matters. Then I gotta wire tellin' me as how Stone and his sidekicks were on the move in a real hurry outa Utah. They been holed up there f' months, so why the sudden move headin' West? Talk had it that somebody had heard Billy Dimond say they were makin' f' a big strike at Bliss. Now that, mister, I found *real* interestin', and I'll tell yuh f' why.'

Logan came to his feet, walked round the room, returned to the table and leaned on it heavily. 'Some time back a shipment of gold left the mine at Carney on its way t' the bank in Bliss. Nothin' unusual in that. The mine was always shippin' out t' Bliss, but there was a difference on this occasion. This was the biggest shipment ever. Close on fifty-thousand dollars' worth.'

Heggerty whistled through clenched teeth.

'Shipment left by wagon with two drivers and half-a-dozen outriders as security. Should've taken three days t' reach Bliss.' Logan paused. 'It never did. Halfway between the mine and here, at a place called Hawk Top, the wagon was attacked, every man-jack of the party killed and the gold spirited away. Never been seen since.'

'Apaches?' asked Heggerty.

'No evidence. No; my reckonin' is that somebody at the mine was workin' with a gang in Bliss. He gave the tip-off, the gang made the raid and the gold was hidden. Still is, waitin' on the day it's safe enough t' start movin' it. The day is close.'

'Yuh mean—' began Heggerty.

'I mean, mister, that them gunslingers are here t' lead a party t' where the gold is stashed. They've been hired as protection at a high price—high enough t' bring them hell-bent outa Utah.'

'But yuh can't prove it,' said Heggerty.

'No, can't prove a thing, not till somebody makes a move. But when them gunslingers do move, I'll be followin'.'

'On yuh own?'

'If that's the way of it.'

Heggerty stood up. 'Seems t' me yuh take this missin' gold a mite personal, Marshal.'

Logan's eyes narrowed. 'I want that gold

returned t' the men who sweated their guts out t' mine it. I want t' bring t' justice the men who attacked the wagon. I want t' know who they are, because one of them killed m' son. He was an outrider with the shipment.'

The two men stared at each other in a silence broken only by the sounds of the street below them.

'Reckon I understand,' said Heggerty.

'Figured yuh f' a fella who...' murmured Logan.

'Even so—' began Heggerty again.

'Even so, I need help—beginnin' with y'self.'

Heggerty frowned. 'Me? How?' he asked.

'Yuh can start by leavin' that Appaloosa right where she is—in the livery.'

'No ways!' snapped Heggerty.

Logan leaned heavily on the table again. 'Figure it out, Heggerty,' he said hoarsely, his blue eyes fading, the creases in his face filling with trickles of sweat. 'If yuh go back t' the livery now, claim yuh horse, what are them gunslingers goin' t' think once they find out, eh? They'll know f'

28

certain yuh didn't die in the desert and that yuh here in Bliss. That could prove embarassin' f' them and whoever it is who's hired them.' He paused. 'Keep things as they are. Let them collect the mare. Let them think they're safe. It's important.'

'What about y'self? How many know yuh in town? Yuh been recognized? Somebody must know yuh here. Joe Pine f' one.'

'I been here two days now and stayed low and outa sight, 'ceptin' f' meetin' up with Joe. He's an old friend from years back. It was Joe who told me about the mare. That's why I been keepin' a watch on her. But Joe owes me. He can be trusted. There's a sheriff by the name of Tranter. I've stayed clear of him so far. Only other person of any note hereabouts is the owner of this hotel, the saloon and just about half the town. A woman. They call her Crystal. Has a spread some ways outa town. Some woman! Red-haired, green-eyed, good-looker and sharp as cactus. Not t' be tangled with. I'm booked in here under the name of Monk.'

Logan eyed Heggerty carefully. 'Well,' he said slowly, 'will yuh help? I sure could do with it right now. And I promise yuh this, Heggerty, we'll get that Appaloosa just as soon as we catch up with them critters.'

'*We?*' frowned Heggerty. 'Yuh expectin' me t' ride with yuh?'

Logan stood back and hooked his thumbs into his waistcoat. 'I'm assumin' yuh wouldn't want t' lose sight of the mare, would yuh?'

Heggerty finished his whiskey in one swift gulp.

THREE

There was a hint of pale dusk, a lengthening of shadows, when Heggerty left the hotel and set off back in the direction of the livery. The street had cleared of its bustle; folk had gone home; the glow of lantern light appeared in windows. Only the saloon blazoned colour, activity and noise. A drunk weaved and wheeled his way towards the store where already the proprietor was locking up. Bliss had had enough for one day.

'And so have I!' murmured Heggerty to himself as he strode on through the still warm dust. Marshal Logan's story had its elements of mystery and intrigue, and maybe he was right—maybe the gunslingers were the key to recovering the gold shipment—but it was his affair, professionally and personally. No place for a stranger. Logan would have to go it alone, or recruit the local sheriff, Heggerty decided. He was certainly not going to risk losing the mare, not after all these years. And as for the bushwhackers—darn it, much as he would relish giving them a whipping, he had, after all, survived. It was time to forget and move on.

He would collect the mare now, however loud Joe Pine's protests, ride back to the Maggs' place to return the bay and pay his respects, and then head clear of the territory.

He could do without Bliss!

He was crossing the street to the livery, his thoughts still recalling Logan's story, when he was suddenly conscious of the darkness surrounding the place. Not a lantern, not a flicker of light. No movements, no sign of Joe Pine. He slowed his pace to a steady walk. A chill of cold sweat had broken in his neck. He held the pace, his eyes dark and watchful, until he was within a few yards of the livery, then bent low and ran into the shadow by the corral fencing.

The bay was still hitched. He frowned;

Joe had made no attempt to tend the mount. He wondered why. His fingers fell lightly to the butt of a Colt. Something was far from right, he thought, then pursed his lips in a low, soft whistle, a sound that would pass unnoticed to the passer-by but one which Heggerty knew the mare would respond to instantly with a gentle snort. Nothing. He tried again. Still nothing. Heggerty's frown deepened. He shifted, moving like a flitting insect through the shadows, closing on the dark interior of the livery.

He slid through the fencing, paused, watching and listening. He felt the first touch of the evening breeze on his cheeks. His eyes narrowed on the darkness as he moved into the livery. Four mounts—and an empty space where the Appaloosa had been.

'Hell!' he cursed, the gunslingers had—

But that was as far as Heggerty's anger went as his eyes adjusted to the gloom and he saw the shape suspended from the rafters beyond the empty space. Joe Pine hung lifeless at the end of a rope, his tongue lolling from his mouth, his eyes bulging like dry grey stones. His hands and feet had been tied.

'Hell!' cursed Heggerty again, took a step forward and stumbled, winced and gasped as something heavy crashed across his shoulders. His head butted the dangling legs of Joe Pine. He heard the creak of the rope as the body began to swing like a giant pendulum, stumbled on to the far wall of the livery, and turned, his eyes watering with the stab of pain.

The figure moving towards him was dark and faceless. There was no hint of features, no eyes, but his hands were huge in their grip on the length of timber. He could hear the coarse rattle of the man's breathing, smell the fetid odour of his breath. The man grunted, lunged, wielded the timber and brought it crashing down on the crouching shape of Heggerty.

But Heggerty had already moved sharply to his right, at the same time lashing out with his boot at the man's legs. There was the crunch of boot on kneecap, a groan from the man as he fell back.

Heggerty plunged after him, his hands scrambling for his throat. The man tossed Heggerty back as if swatting a fly from his shirt, dropped the timber and reached for his gun.

His draw was cumbersome, laboured and uncertain, too slow to match Heggerty's lightning flick of his fingers to his right-hand Colt. The man must have seen the blaze of the gun before his trigger finger had touched metal and felt the burning sear of lead in his gut in the split-second later. He reeled, spun, fell into the swinging body of Joe Pine and was booted to the left by the corpse.

He was as dead as Joe when he hit the floor.

Heggerty took a deep breath, wiped the sweat from his brow and staggered towards the fresh air. Who the hell had attacked him, and why? Was the man he had just shot Joe Pine's killer? But why had the livery owner had to die, and where was the mare? Time for Marshal Josh Logan to answer a few questions, he reckoned!

Heggerty had slipped from the livery to

the early evening glow when he saw the glint of a Winchester barrel protruding through the fencing. Its aim was steady and levelled at his chest. He halted, peered ahead, then swung round, his hands on his gun butts at the sound of a voice from the shadows.

'Hold it, mister. Don't move another muscle.'

It was a round-shouldered, slightly stooped bulk of a man that walked slowly into the glow. His face was creased, pitted, a fixed grin slanting from his thin lips, his eyes no more than slits beneath the dark outcrop of eyebrows. His sheriff's badge and his drawn Colt glinted in the light.

'Yuh been havin' y'self a busy time, mister!' he said, a squat deputy sliding to his side. 'But that's as far as it goes.' The grin broadened.

'Steady up, Sheriff,' began Heggerty, 'I came here—'

'I can see clear enough why yuh came here!' The sheriff spat violently into the sand. 'I'm takin' yuh in f' the murder of Joe Pine and the killin' of Sam Merrett.

36

Yuh'll hang f' this, sure as hell's fire yuh will!'

'Just a minute—' began Heggerty again.

'Yuh got anythin' t' say, yuh can save it f' the Judge.'

Heggerty's mouth opened. He was about to mention the marshall's name, to explain about the mare, the gunslingers, Logan's reasons for being in Bliss, but maybe not here, he thought, not in front of the deputies and within earshot of the straggling of folk who had gathered in the street at the sound of gunfire. No, not here. This was not the place. He would have to go along with the sheriff.

He shrugged and offered no resistance when the deputy disarmed him.

'Let's go,' said the sheriff, and gestured with his Colt towards the jail.

Sheriff Tranter leaned back on the wall, folded his arms and stared at Heggerty from the other side of the cell bars.

'No question of it, mister, yuh goin' t' hang—high as they come!' His slanting lips twisted to a grin. His eyes clouded. 'That was a mean killin' yuh did back there, mister. Sonofabitch mean! But don't fret none, yuh'll know just how Joe Pine felt when it comes t' yuh own turn f' hangin'! And that can't come soon enough in my book. Just as soon as Judge Boone hits the territory. Three days from now. And yuh can take it from me, he don't waste no time when it comes t' killers. He'll have yuh hangin' inside the week!'

'There's a marshal in town,' said Heggerty flatly. 'Yuh'd best get him here. He'll explain.'

Tranter's grin broadened to a smile. 'A marshal, eh? And which marshal might that be?'

'Marshal Josh Logan,' said Heggerty impatiently. 'I been with him most of the afternoon at the hotel. I know why he's here. He's been trackin' four gunslingers—they bushwhacked me—and like as not they killed Joe Pine and took my mare. They probably got a two-hour start on us, so cut the secrecy, Sheriff, and let's move it!'

Tranter laughed. 'I'll say this f' yuh,

mister, yuh sure got an imagination! S'pose these gunslingers shot Sam Merrett in passin', eh?'

'No, I shot him. He jumped me in the livery. No idea why. Never set eyes on the fella before. Now will yuh—'

'Which marshal was that again?' growled Tranter.

Heggerty sighed. 'Marshal Josh Logan. At the hotel. Room ten.'

'Marshal Logan, eh? Well, now ain't that somethin'. Marshal Josh Logan... Yuh sure about that?'

''Course I'm sure!' snapped Heggerty, his impatience festering.

Tranter stared hard at Heggerty. 'Yuh been drinkin', mister?' he asked softly.

'Drinkin'! F'Crissake, sheriff—'

'Seein' things mebbe?'

Heggerty frowned. The sweat in his neck was cold and clinging.

'Or mebbe yuh just plain flipped. Yeah, crazy as a cracked rattler!' said Tranter, his face suddenly expressionless. 'Know somethin', mister, yuh a darned fool liar! Marshal Josh Logan's been dead close

39

on twelve months. Got himself shot up somewhere back East. Marshal Logan ain't no more than bones buried deep more than a hundred miles from here. So who'd yuh reckon's takin' up space in room ten, eh? His ghost?'

Heggerty paced the length of his cell, reached the blank wall, stared at it, turned and paced back. How in tarnation had he got into this situation, he grimaced? Had he been duped, bushwhacked yet again, set up like some dumb stooge—but for what purpose and to what end? Who was the man who claimed to be Marshal Logan? Was somebody impersonating him? But why? And why had Joe Pine had to die? And what had Sam Merrett been doing at the livery? More important, where was the mysterious marshal now? Where were the gunslingers, where was the mare—and how in hell was he going to get out of this cage?

He turned again, leaned on the cell bars and wiped the sweat from his face. He had no hope of persuading Sheriff Tranter to

40

verify his story. He would wager a full hand that room ten at the hotel was now empty, and just as full a hand that the gunslingers had long since cleared Bliss. Charlie Maggs and Joni would vouch for the fact that Heggerty had walked out of the desert, but that was all they could vouch for. That, he reckoned, left him with precisely nothing!

He raised his head at the sound of Sheriff Tranter's voice in the room beyond the cells.

'Takin' an hour f' supper, Jake,' he called to the turnkey. 'I'll be at the saloon. Yuh just keep a close eye on that murderin' critter, OK?'

The turnkey grunted. The door to the sheriffs office banged shut and the night silence descended.

Heggerty went to his bunk, sat down and cradled his chin in his hands. It was time for some careful thinking...

Heggerty was still deep in thought a half-hour later when he stirred at the sound of a new voice in the office. He came slowly to his feet. No mistaking whose voice it

41

was. So Marshal Josh Logan had arrived at last!

Heggerty walked to the cell bars, gripped them and waited.

FOUR

The door to the cell block opened slowly. Heggerty peered into the glow of brighter light. He saw the greasy, sweat-streaked face of the turnkey, a look of bewilderment widening his eyes, and behind him, a Colt levelled at the turnkey's back, the tall, dark figure of Logan. He glanced quickly at Heggerty, then prodded the turnkey forward. Heggerty made to speak, but uttered no sound. If Logan was here in his official capacity as a marshal, he sure had a strange way of showing it!

'Open up,' snapped Logan.

The turnkey fumbled nervously with a bunch of keys. 'Yuh ain't got no hope of gettin' away with this, mister,' he mouthed miserably. 'I'm telling yuh now—'

'Just do it!' snapped Logan again.

The turnkey slid the key to the lock, turned it and opened the cell door.

Heggerty stood silent and motionless, his mind swimming with a score of questions. What the hell was going on?

'Out,' said Logan, gesturing to Heggerty with the Colt.

'Yuh'll not get a mile before—' began the turnkey, and then fell forward into the cell and collapsed with a throaty grunt under the crushing blow of Logan's gun across the back of his head.

'Get yuh Colts and let's go!' said Logan, slamming the cell door shut, locking it and pocketing the key. 'There's two mounts out back. Move it!' His blue eyes gleamed in an unblinking stare.

'What in tarnation—' hissed Heggerty.

'Questions and answers later,' clipped Logan. 'Now shift yuh butt, and fast!'

Minutes later, Logan and Heggerty were riding hard out of Bliss in a cloud of dust that shimmered on the night like midges. They cleared the town without pausing, and there was no easing of the pace when Logan veered suddenly eastwards deep into the silent darkness.

Heggerty's thoughts whirled as his eyes

44

narrowed against the cool sting of the night air. Why had Logan sprung him? Where were they heading? Was the man crouched in the saddle at his side really Marshal Josh Logan? But if he was not Logan, then who the hell was he?

They had crossed a spread of open plain, brushed through the fringes of a cluster of trees, topped a ridge and clattered at a slower rate into the loose shale and rock of a gulley before Logan reined up, wiped a hand across his face and adjusted his hat.

'This goes deeper,' he said hoarsely. 'We'll go as deep as it comes, then wait.' He moved on without another word as if having spoken to himself.

The gulley continued to shelve steeply, a slithering slope of stones and screes that finally dropped to a dry-bed stream locked in on both sides by walls of sheer rock face. Here, the night was deeper, darker, the shadows thicker and stiffer in the starry light.

'Far enough,' said Logan, dismounting and leading his mount into the cool of the rock face.

Heggerty followed, then turned sharply on Logan. 'Don't get mistakin' me, Marshal,' he said, his gaze searching Logan's face. 'I'm grateful t' yuh f' springin' me back there. Sheriff had got the whole situation round his neck, and time is what I need t' prove I didn't kill Joe Pine. Reckon I know well enough who did, though—but that ain't m' point.' He paused and came a step closer to Logan. 'Tranter reckons yuh don't exist, that yuh died somewhere back East. So if Marshal Josh Logan is dead, who the hell are you, why did yuh spin me that yarn this afternoon, and why am I here?'

Logan was silent for a moment, his stare fixed in a time and space far beyond the gulley, then he began to smile, at first softly, slowly, until his face creased in a wide grin and he chuckled throatily.

'Well, ain't that somethin'!' he laughed. 'Just fancy that—me dead! Worked like a charm! Never thought it would, but, darn m' hide, it sure as hell did!'

'Riddles,' grunted Heggerty. 'Yuh talkin' in riddles.'

46

Logan's smile faded. 'Yuh right, mister. Must seem like that from where yuh standin'.'

'That's a fact!' spat Heggerty.

'T'ain't easy goin' back,' began Logan, his voice lower, easier, 'but I owe it t' yuh now.' He glanced anxiously at Heggerty. 'Sure I died out East, leastways that's what I wanted folk t' think, and it seems like they did. I had good reason t' die.'

He paused. 'Like I told yuh, m' son was ridin' guard on that gold shipment outa Carney. It was John's first real job. He was just eighteen. Fine boy. Full of spirit, like his ma, I guess. I didn't want him t' take the job, but he'd grown kinda independent and self-willed since Corah died.' Logan paused again as if moving among images long since lost. 'Anyhow, he joined up with the team leavin' Carney f' Bliss. I was none too happy, but it sometimes don't do f' a father t' go round wearin' his feelin's on his sleeve. Do more harm than good. But that didn't stop me from keepin' an eye on things. I could do that easy enough as marshal. Trouble was, I was just an

47

hour, one lousy, goddamn hour, too late in reachin' Hawk Top on that day.'

Logan's eyes were suddenly wet and dull. 'I was delayed, holed up at Black Peaks bringin' in a couple of horse thieves. It was long after noon when I reached Hawk Top. Planned on just takin' a look from a distance. Didn't want the boy t' think I was wet-nursin' him. But by the time I arrived, the raid was over. There was nothin' but charred remains of the wagon, the men, horses... Whoever had done that job had set fire t' all that was left. Nothin' recognizable.' Logan sighed, wiped his face, cleared his throat. 'Don't mind tellin' yuh I just stood there in that black dirt and the stench of burned flesh and broke up like a babe. My wife gone and now m' son. Then, when the sorrowin' was done, I got t' bein' angry, real angry! Blood boilin'! If it took all the life left t' me, I vowed I'd get them critters. Shoot 'em down like vermin! Question was—how?

'I figured it'd soon be known that Marshal Logan's son had been killed in the raid, and that, I reckoned, would put the whole scurvy bunch on their guard. Mebbe I'd never get close t' them. Mouths close when a marshal starts askin'. Fact that the gold seemed t' have disappeared suggested that whoever had lifted it was in no hurry t' use it. So, if Marshal Josh Logan wasn't around...I decided t' quit bein' marshal. I'd head East, lose m'self and m' identity. Marshal Logan.wouldn't exist. I became plain Frank Monk.

'Wasn't difficult spreadin' rumours that I'd died. Joe Pine helped there. I kept contact with him and he soon put it about Bliss that I'd finally caught m' number in a gunfight. All I had t' do then was wait. I was still convinced that the raid on the shipment had been organized outa Bliss. Sooner or later, somebody would make a move f' that hidden gold. Then I heard about Stone's shift outa Utah headin' f' Bliss. That, I reckoned, was it. The rest yuh know.'

''Ceptin' my part in all this,' grunted Heggerty.

'Accidental,' said Logan. 'Joe told me

about the mare. Figured yuh'd come f' it, and yuh did. Soon as I clapped eyes on yuh I knew I'd found the man likely to help. Reckon yuh still will too. No use t' me in jail, though, so I sprung yuh. Yuh gotta clear yuh name over that killin' at the livery, and yuh sure as hell want that Appaloosa under yuh butt again.'

Heggerty sighed. 'Looks as if I walked right int' a rattler's nest!' He slapped his mount's saddle. 'Don't look t' have a deal of choice, do I? But who the hell was Sam Merrett? I don't figure he killed Pine. So just what was he doin' at Joe's place? He tied in with them gunslingers?'

'Can't say. All I know about Merrett is that he was a hired hand f' that woman I mentioned—Crystal. He was no close friend of Joe's, that's f' sure.'

Heggerty sighed again. 'What now?' he asked. 'Tranter ain't goin' t' take kindly t' yuh springin' me. There'll be a posse movin' come first light.'

Logan grunted. 'We make f' Hawk Top. That gold's hidden somewhere near there.

Gotta be. And Stone and his boys'll know it. That's where we begin.'

'But not before I been back t' the Maggs place. I owe them that much,' said Heggerty flatly.

'Risky and time-wastin',' said Logan.

'The Maggs place!' snapped Heggerty. 'That's north. Let's go!'

They rode quietly, carefully along the reach of the gulley, the night closing in on them like a cloak. There were no further words spoken between them. No need, thought Heggerty, most of it had been said. He could either believe Logan's story or dismiss it; either way, it still left him with a sheriff and his posse sitting on his tail and the mare in the hands of Stone and his sidekicks.

It also left him with a prickly trickle of sweat in his neck that warned instinctively that all was not as it should be, that maybe Logan had still not told him the full story, that maybe he was being used in the unfolding of it.

He glanced quickly at the man as they

broke into a pool of moonlight. Nothing in his eyes that mirrored shifty or uncertain thoughts. Nothing uneasy in the set of his chin, the firm hands on the reins. Josh Logan seemed resolved and set to his purpose. Kill or be killed. He perhaps had nothing to lose. His loss lay in the death of his wife and, maybe worse, in the black burned dirt of Hawk Top where the wind had blown the last dust of his son to oblivion. No telling, Heggerty guessed, how deep the darkness of Logan's thoughts. No telling who might ever know them, or where they were leading.

They had cleared the gulley in less than an hour and now, in the chill thin of the night air, turned north. The country was featureless, with only the slim drift of knolls and rocky outcrops for cover. But they moved confidently, safe in the reckoning that Tranter would not raise a posse until sun-up, but equally certain that when he did and made his move he would have no difficulty picking up their trail. It would be all cat and mouse from here to Hawk Top.

Another half-hour and they were into a steady canter across open desert approaching the Maggs spread. The few shapes ahead of them stood stark and black, still and silent. Only the scuff of the mounts' hooves through sand stirred the land in its sleep. Heggerty wished he could share it. His eyes were heavy with tiredness, his body still aching and chafed from the ordeal of his desert crossing, and his thoughts a confusion of events that made little sense.

But not so confused that he failed to spot the sudden soft glow of light from a window as they closed on the Maggs home. He slowed his mount and was conscious of Logan riding easy at his side.

'They keep late hours,' murmured Logan. 'Or sit up with the ghosts!'

Heggerty's gaze hardened on the glow. Maybe Joni was still about; maybe the old man could not sleep. Maybe something else, he thought, as he reined the mount to an abrupt halt, laid a hand on Logan's arm and narrowed his eyes on the shape that had moved through the glow to the fencing ahead of them.

He had yet to see the ghost that could level a steady Winchester.

FIVE

'Give me cover and I could drop him from here,' whispered Logan, reaching to the scabbard for his rifle.

'Hold it,' said Heggerty, his hands tightening on the reins. 'Reckon that's the Indian fella workin' f' Maggs. He's got trouble. Move real slow.'

They walked the mounts on gently, the creak and squeak of leather echoing on the empty night air, their eyes fixed on the dark, moonlit shape of the figure at the fence, the unmoving level of the barrel.

Heggerty had caught only a brief glimpse of the Apache hand they called Tentrees during his stay at the homestead. He had seen him saddling the bay, waved a hand to him as he had set off for Bliss. It had been no more than a fleeting image of the man: medium height but muscular, raven-black, shoulder-length hair banded

55

at the forehead, belted smock and baggy pants; a still and silent man whose dark eyes watched without a flicker of emotion, revealing nothing, alive to everything.

No doubt about it, the man at the fence was Tentrees. No doubt either that he was in a shooting mood.

Heggerty moved a pace or so ahead of Logan, raised himself in the saddle and waved. 'Tentrees—it's me, Heggerty,' he called. 'We're comin' in.'

He sat easy again and narrowed his eyes on the silhouetted shape beyond the glow from the window. If the Indian was going to shoot he would do it now with Heggerty walking his mount deliberately into range. The rifle barrel stayed steady, the aim deadly. Heggerty felt the cold prickle of sweat in his neck. 'Slow now. Slow,' he murmured to the mount.

The rifle barrel shifted a fraction towards Logan; shifted again, back to Heggerty, then slowly as if being swallowed on the night lowered and disappeared. The Indian waited.

Heggerty came to within a few feet of

the fence, halted and stared at Tentrees. The Apache's eyes were cold, unblinking, speaking words that found no voice. A wound on his forehead oozed a trickle of blood. He stood back, nodded and indicated for Heggerty to follow him into the home.

'Goddamnit!' muttered Logan at Heggerty's back as they slowly hitched their mounts. 'Just plain goddamnit!'

Heggerty blinked and shielded his eyes against the glare from a lantern in the homestead's main living-room. He saw a chaos of upturned furniture, scatterings from half-open drawers, thrown aside pots, pans and, gleamingly ridiculous in a pool of stew, a shattered porcelain figure of some grand eastern lady, a ripped shirt of the colour he was certain Joni had been wearing—and breathless and heaving in a corner of the room, a bloodstain spreading from his gut, the sprawled, limp frame of Charlie Maggs.

Heggerty dropped to one knee at the old man's side and touched his arm lightly.

'Charlie,' he murmured. 'F' Crissake, what happened? How'd—'

Maggs retched painfully, his body contorted, but slowly, like the lifting of frail, broken blinds, his eyes opened, focused and settled in a soft gaze on Heggerty's face.

'Four,' he hissed. 'Them gunslingers...' He retched again, his face creasing in the agony of pain. 'They got Joni... Took her.' A shaking, claw-shaped hand reached for Heggerty's shirt. 'Yuh do something f' me, mister?'

'Sure,' said Heggerty.

'Yuh go get Joni? Yuh get them lice? Do it f' me, mister. Yuh do that?'

Heggerty felt a cold, slithering shiver down his spine. 'Yuh got it, Charlie.'

The old man's lips moved in a tremor of a grin. 'Knew yuh would. Knew it...said yuh'd be back...'

Logan eased to Heggerty's side. 'He needs a doc fast.'

'Too late f' that,' murmured Heggerty, and watched as Charlie Maggs's breathing gathered in a sudden violent spasm, pitched

58

like a tide, and ebbed until the body was empty and the life gone.

Heggerty cursed softly, closed the man's eyes and, coming to his feet, turned to face Tentrees. 'How long back?' he asked drily, his gaze as fierce as the set of his lips.

'Three hours. They came quiet. No noise. Like shadows. Seemed like they knew the place. Knew what they were coming for. I saw them first, out there by the fence. But there was no time to do anything. No fight. The big one, he clubbed me to the ground, then there was nothing, only darkness, until I came to and found this—Miss Joni gone and Charlie dying. There was no chance for him. He would not let me leave him. He knew the long sleep was close.'

'Lucky they didn't do f' you,' muttered Logan.

'They take much?' asked Heggerty.

Tentrees grunted. 'They came only for Miss Joni.' His eyes flashed.

'Cy Bennett's doin',' said Logan.

The Indian moved past Heggerty and knelt by the old man's body. 'I will take care of Charlie. I will bury him as he wished, where he will see the sun come up. It was as he wanted.'

Logan walked to the open door and gestured for Heggerty to join him. 'We gotta move,' he said softly. 'Can't hang about here. Them scum are a good four hours ahead by now and Tranter'll be movin' in just one.'

'Yuh reckon they planned this all along?' asked Heggerty.

Logan shrugged. 'Bennett never could resist a woman. The others—they're dirt, mister. He'd have had no trouble in persuadin' them t' grab the girl. God help her!'

The sweat in Heggerty's neck turned colder.

'Say yuh piece t' the Indian and let's move it,' said Logan. 'I'll go see t' the mounts.'

Heggerty turned back to Tentrees. 'Yuh need a hand?'

'No,' said Tentrees, still tending the body. 'I will do it.'

Heggerty waited in silence for a moment

until the Indian came to his feet.

'You will do as Charlie wished?' asked Tentrees. 'You will bring Miss Joni back?'

Heggerty nodded and grunted.

'Good. She is a fine woman. I think much of her. We have been here many years. Charlie was as a father to us. We owe him much.' His dark eyes were suddenly hard as if fired to stone. 'You know the men who came here?'

'Not well enough yet,' said Heggerty harshly. 'But I gotta fancy we're goin' t' get real close.'

'It will happen,' said Tentrees. 'It will be so.' And then he turned again to the body and stared at it. 'The spirit will move with you. It is already so. You must watch for the man who trails the Appaloosa. When you face this man you will feel the spirit.'

Heggerty took a last look at the drained grey face of Charlie Maggs, the torn shirt his niece had worn, and without another word went silently from the homestead.

He saw nothing of the gaze that followed him, nothing of the Apache's eyes and the light that had filled them.

The cold sweat in the nape of Heggerty's neck had turned to a trickle of ice in spite of the still warm air of the desert in that slow hour summoning dawn. He rode easy a pace or so behind Logan on the sweep of sands to the north of Charlie Maggs's home.

Dammit, there had been no need for the old man to end his days like that. No sonofabitch reason at all... And in that same moment, and maybe for the hundredth time, the images of Charlie's last breath, the strange reality of recognition in his staring eyes, had faded, only to be replaced by those of Joni being taken by Cy Bennett, manhandled by the others, her shirt torn away, her young body leered at, snatched at, grabbed before the four had bundled her on to a mount and ridden on.

Goddammit, he owed his life to the girl!

The sweat turned warmer, tighter, blood-boiled to anger.

He glanced at the dark shape of Logan's back. He had shown little emotion at what they had found at the homestead. No shock, no anger, no disgust for a pointless death, no anxiety for the fate awaiting Joni Maggs. His only concern had been to stay ahead of Tranter and his posse. Maybe Logan had seen too much of death and degradation to let it bother him, save when it was as close as the killing of his own son. Maybe he was obsessed with the tracking down of Emmett Stone and his sidekicks. Maybe even now, as he rode purposefully into the gathering light of day, he saw nothing but the ghosts of the dead at Hawk Top and the faces of those he planned would soon join them.

Heggerty tightened his hands on the reins and cursed again. Cursed his decision days ago to take a look at Bliss; cursed his mistake that night of bedding down in the cottonwoods—and cursed himself for not taking Joni Maggs' advice and resting up at the homestead, for riding into Bliss too soon and walking into Josh Logan's life.

His hands tightened again at the thought of Tentrees in his lonely work of burying the old man, and the sweat in his neck ran colder at the memory of the Indian's words. *'The spirit will move with you.'*

That, he reckoned, was Apache talk.

The morning was a splash of white light in a sprawl of amber sunglow when Logan reined his mount westwards and pointed to the spread of a mountain range in the far distance. He waited for Heggerty to draw alongside him.

'T'ain't goin' t' fool Tranter none, we're leavin' too much trail, but if we hit them rocks it's goin' t' slow him down some. Posse don't move easy in rough country.'

Heggerty grunted and tipped the brim of his hat.

'There's a track up there that drops int' Loosewater Plain. We'll hole-up there an hour or so. My guess is Stone'll mebbe take the same trail, unless he's got a meetin' with his bosses planned somewheres else. We'll see.' Logan glanced anxiously at Heggerty. 'Yuh frettin' over that girl.'

'Wouldn't be around 'ceptin' f' her,' said Heggerty. 'Owe m' life t' her.'

Logan stared ahead. 'Let's hope she holds on to hers,' he muttered coldly.

Heggerty urged his mount to a faster pace and drew clear of Logan.

They walked the mounts carefully over the stone and screes track that climbed the eastern side of the range. Now the light was brighter and bolder, throwing long shadows from the shelvings and clusters of rocks, the heat of the day already thickening. Twice they paused to stare back over the desert they had left. There was no hint of Tranter and his posse, not so much as a dust cloud of movement.

'He don't seem t' be in a sweatin' hurry,' said Logan, turning again to the track.

They climbed on. In a half-hour they had swung away from the track into a clutch of steeper rocks. The shadows tightened, the air was cooler, the sound of the mounts' hooves on stone echoing eerily. Heggerty halted to wipe the sweat from his brow as they cleared the narrower end of the gully.

He raised his eyes to the higher crags and the shimmer of the sun's glare.

'We ain't alone,' he murmured as Logan stepped to his side. 'Up there.'

They shaded their eyes and peered to the high rocks and the shape silhouetted on the skyline.

Tentrees raised an arm in recognition.

SIX

'How the hell he get here so fast?' muttered Logan as he struggled with Heggerty to lead the mounts over the last few yards to the rim of the crag. 'And why's he here, anyhow?'

Heggerty smiled quietly to himself. He was tempted to remind Logan that no real explanation ever came of questioning Indian thinking and doing, leastways not to white reckoning, but he could make a fair guess at Tentrees' reasoning since the bushwhackers' assault on the homestead. If the death of Charlie Maggs had not been enough to raise his Apache blood, the taking of Joni had left no doubt in his mind as to what he had to do.

'Wouldn't argue the point if I were you,' was Heggerty's only comment as they came to within a few yards of the still seated Indian.

Tentrees made no attempt to move as Logan and Heggerty drew closer. He watched them as a hawk might follow its prey, but there was no emotion in his face. Heggerty reckoned he had been watching them for maybe nearly an hour. Strange truth was that he had known exactly where to wait for them.

Heggerty sat at his side, but said nothing while his gaze roved over the tumble of rocks to the sweep of the valley and plain below him. Scrub and sand country swept clean to a higher mountain range to the north. Lonely country, he thought, the sort a man might cross heading nowhere. He turned his gaze to Tentrees.

'We gotta posse sittin' on our tails,' he said. 'Spot of bother back in Bliss. Yuh catch any sight of them?'

'No posse,' said Tentrees.

Heggerty grunted. His gaze went back to the plain. 'Any others?'

'Five riders crossed in the night.'

Heggerty stiffened. 'The bushwhackers? Miss Joni?'

Tentrees nodded.

'That's it!' snapped Logan. 'We're close. Let's move!'

'One still here,' said the Indian. 'The old one.'

'Slocum!' Logan snapped a flat hand on a rock. 'Where? Where's he holed-up?'

'Where mebbe ain't so important as why,' said Heggerty.

Tentrees turned his gaze on Heggerty. 'Right,' he said. 'Why? I am asking the same.' He paused and narrowed his gaze on the far northern mountains. 'He waits up there. Alone. In a cave.'

'He's mine!' croaked Logan, moving to his mount.

'Wait!' Heggerty came to his feet. 'This needs figurin'.'

'Figurin' be darned!' Logan grabbed impatiently at his mount's reins. 'There ain't no figurin' t' be done. Slocum's out there and we got him cold. I ain't interested in why!'

'Mebbe yuh should be,' said Heggerty slowly. 'One question: why should Stone leave Slocum here and ride on with the others? There's gotta be a reason. Ain't no sense t' it otherwise.'

'He waits for someone,' said Tentrees standing up.

'F' Crissakes, who?' flared Logan.

'Suggest we find out,' said Heggerty.

'Yuh mean just sit around waitin'?' asked Logan.

'Slocum ain't squattin' in a cave f' his health,' said Heggerty. 'He's plannin' on meetin' somebody. Seems t' me it's likely that whoever that somebody is must be tied in with the gold. We need t' know who.'

Logan sighed. 'Mebbe. But if Slocum gets away—'

'He won't,' said Heggerty.

'What about the girl?' persisted Logan. 'The longer she's with them scum...'

'I don't rest easy with the thought, mister. As far as I'm concerned—'

Tentrees laid a hand on Heggerty's shoulder and pointed to the far western drift of the plain and the slow swirl of a growing blur of dust. 'Two riders,' he said quietly. 'In a hurry.'

'T'ain't Tranter's men,' murmured Logan. 'Wrong direction.'

Heggerty narrowed his eyes on the cloud. No doubt about it the riders were heading for the mountain range. For the cave? He swung his gaze to the shadowed bulks of the rock faces. No sign of Slocum, but he could not have failed to see the cloud—not if he was expecting company.

'Hold on here,' said Heggerty firmly. 'I'm goin' t' move round t' them caves. I wanna take a good look at Slocum's visitors.'

Logan opened his mouth to speak, but stayed silent under Heggerty's stare.

'The cave is halfway up the short face to the east,' said Tentrees.

Heggerty grunted and began to lead his mount back down the gully. 'Give me an hour,' he said without turning.

A gap in the loose rocks at the lower end of the gully was wide enough for Heggerty and his mount to turn north. Once clear of its rough going he was able to canter through a more open area of sand and stone, scattered scrub and the few bare bones of petrified trees. Sparse cover, but

71

sufficient perhaps to keep him hidden from Slocum's view.

He moved into a scramble of heavier rocks; sand gave way to a sudden scattering of shale and for a moment he was fearful of its echoing clatter as the mount struggled for a foothold. But now, as the rock faces tightened again, he could make out the darker smudges of the caves, their gaping mouths, the slopes of the ledges fronting them.

He reined up, dismounted, tethered the mount and climbed into the rocks. He went higher, clinging to the surfaces like a fly, clawed his way into shadow, paused, wiped the sweat from his eyes and raised his head above a rim of jagged granite.

The two riders were within a hundred yards of the mountain screes and already slowing as they scanned the caves for a sight of Slocum. The leading rider was stocky, broad-shouldered, heavy with muscles, his eyes like bright white lights beneath the wide brim of his hat. His partner was younger, leaner, sallow-faced and fidgety, the fingers of his right hand playing constantly over the butt of his holstered Colt.

The two riders came on, reined back their mounts to a canter then a walk. The horses snorted, tack jangled, leather creaked. The heftier man finally pulled up, mopped his brow and ran his gaze slowly over the rock faces. The younger man drew to his side, but continued to fidget, his nerves coiled, his eyes flicking to left and right. Heggerty watched and waited.

It was a full minute before Slocum appeared at the mouth of the cave nearest to Heggerty. He cradled a Winchester in his arms and stared hard at the two riders.

'Yuh made it OK?' said the leading rider. 'No trouble?'

'None we couldn't handle.' Slocum's voice was a slow, southern drawl, colourless, humourless. A man of few words, thought Heggerty. He would shoot first and leave the talking to the talkers.

'Yuh all set?' asked the hefty rider.

Slocum grunted. 'Y'selves?'

73

'Boss sent us on t' be sure yuh were here.'

'I ain't no ghost,' drawled Slocum.

'Tranter'll be here soon. No tellin' when. Mebbe a day, no more than two. Yuh just be sure yuh here, Slocum. Yuh know what t' do. Yuh all clear in yuh mind? Boss says no mistakes.'

'I ain't deaf.' Slocum spat into the dirt.

'We're ridin' on t' Hawk Top. Rest'll be there come sundown. We head f' Carney at first light.'

Slocum grunted again.

'Where's Stone?'

'Around,' said Slocum. 'He'll be there when he's needed.'

The riders watched Slocum carefully for a moment, then reined their mounts' heads to the north. 'We'll see yuh soon.'

'Give m' best t' Crystal,' grinned Slocum.

'Yuh can bet!' called the riders as they turned and set a fast pace into open land.

Heggerty, his fingers sore from gripping the rock face, his arms and legs spread like

74

the limbs of a basking lizard, dropped his head and lay painfully flat.

Crystal—the woman Logan had described as sharp as cactus, the big wheel in Bliss—was she the 'boss' who had planned the raid on the gold shipment? Was she out there now leading a team to recover it?

And how deep was Tranter's involvement? Deep enough to explain why he had been so anxious to jail Heggerty. But had he mounted a posse, or was his rendezvous here with Slocum more important?

Heggerty sighed and blinked away the sweat in his eyes. What seemed certain was that the gold was somewhere in Carney, but less easy to fathom was the whereabouts of Stone and the rest of the gunslingers. His eyes narrowed, his lips tightened at the thought of what might be happening to Joni Maggs. Maybe it was time for Slocum to be a mite more talkative...

He slid gently from the rim and crouched in the shadowed overhang of rock. His fingers tapped lightly on the butts of his twin Colts as he considered how best to work his way to the cave.

There was a way...over the top and down to his right where he had noticed the shale ledge fronting the cave was at its widest.

He climbed again, this time moving quickly through a tumble of sharp crags and smooth, brooding boulders until, sprawled flat on his stomach, he was able to look down on the mouth of the cave. There was no sight or sound of Slocum. He moved to his right, waited a moment, then picked his way slowly towards the shale ledge.

He had both feet on it and had paused again when he saw the glint of the rifle barrel in the gloom of the cave; a glint that was as sudden and watchful as a waking eye. Seconds that seemed like long minutes passed before the barrel edged forward and came to life behind the grinning bulk of Slocum.

'Well, now,' he sneered, 'I reckon I got m'self an interloper!' He took a firm step into the brighter light, his fingers hardening on the Winchester. 'Heard yuh comin', mister. Yuh get t' hearin' good if yuh wanna stay alive.'

And that, reckoned Heggerty, was about

76

as much as he was going to hear from Slocum, judging by the steadily glazing stare in his eyes, the fading grin, the concentration on the sheer efficiency of killing quickly. Men of few words rarely asked questions.

Heggerty's thoughts raced. One twitch of a finger, the lift of an eyebrow, a deeper breath, and the rifle barrel would blaze its fire. He had only one chance, and a half-second to grab it.

Heggerty flung himself from the ledge in a violent flight of arms and legs. But even as he moved, and before he had begun to fall, the Winchester spat, save that now Heggerty was no longer a sitting target. He felt the heat of the shot scorch his ribs as he fell back into the space beyond the ledge, but his eyes had never left Slocum's face, the face he had imagined a thousand times in that long, parched struggle across the desert and had leered like a haunting before he finally collapsed. Nor had Heggerty's fingers been idle.

They had clamoured instinctively for a Colt, found its butt, closed on it and drawn the gun as he toppled into whatever abyss awaited.

And now his own barrel spat its vengeance; a single shot, like a last, raging curse. It found Slocum's shoulder, spun him round and back into the cave as Heggerty disappeared from his sight.

Heggerty hit shale, bounced and slithered as if tossed to the surface of the earth in some dark eruption. When he finally stopped, his back lodged against a ridge of rock, he squinted into the sunlight, at the shadow-swathed shape of Slocum staggering precariously on the rim of the ledge. The Winchester roared wildly. Heggerty's Colt spat again, and through the sweat that clouded his eyes he watched the old gunslinger fall like a rock to the shale and slide on and past him to the hot dirt of the desert.

In less than a minute there were flies on Slocum's dead, staring eyes.

SEVEN

'Goddammit, Heggerty, yuh tellin' me that Tranter's been tied up in this all along, that he's in with that bitch, Crystal, that he's known right from the start?'

'I'm tellin' yuh what I heard,' said Heggerty, wiping a water-soaked rag over his face, then staring at Logan.

Logan pushed his hat to the back of his head and kicked angrily at a loose stone. 'Don't make a mite of sense.'

'Fact is, Tranter ain't goin' t' find Slocum waitin' f' him when he gets here. Where's that goin' t' leave him? What'll he do? Has he raised a posse t' trail us, or has he mebbe found some good reason f' sittin' tight in Bliss till the time comes t' ride out t' Slocum? Posse should've been close by now by m' reckonin', *if* it ever got mounted.'

They stood in silence in the shadow of

the rock face for a moment and gazed at the stiff, fly-crusted body of the gunslinger. Tentrees squatted on his haunches in the full glare of the sun a few yards away, his slim fingers trickling pebbles from one hand to the other, his eyes narrowed and steady on the shimmering heat-haze of the plain.

'Yuh should've left Slocum f' me,' muttered Logan.

'Didn't have a deal of choice at the time,' said Heggerty, running the rag round his neck. 'He wasn't exactly the waitin' sort.'

Logan grunted. 'Still leaves three.'

Heggerty tied the rag at his throat, replaced his hat and hitched his Colts higher. 'Yuh can take yuh pick when the time comes, Logan. Meantime, we got some plannin' t' do. Yuh given any thought t' that?'

Logan sighed. 'Just can't figure—'

'Let's quit the speculatin' and get t' movin'. Way I see it we gotta f'get Tranter f' now—he's goin' t' be here sooner or later, anyhow—find Stone and Joni Maggs and get closer t' Carney. I figure it's best f' you t' head f' Carney, find out what yuh can and stay low.'

'And you?' asked Logan.

'I'm goin' t' join up with Miss Crystal and her party.'

Logan's eyes flashed. 'Yuh gonna what?'

Heggerty wiped the back of his hand across his mouth. 'She and her party don't know me. Figure I can mebbe work m' way int' ridin' with her and find out where Stone's holed up.'

'Don't reckon she'd let yuh within spittin' distance of her,' snapped Logan.

'I'll take that chance,' said Heggerty bluntly.

Logan sighed again. 'And the Indian here? I suppose yuh got it all figured f' him too?'

'He'll trail me. Outa sight, but close enough t' get clear back t' you if it all goes wrong. Agreed?'

'Yuh takin' on somethin', yuh know that? Yuh ain't given a thought—'

'I done all the thinkin' I'm doin' f' now. I didn't ask t' get int' this—can't rightly figure how I did—but now I'm in, I'm handlin' things my way. Yuh keep yuh mind on that gold and whatever else concerns yuh. Me—I'm goin' t' get Joni Maggs outa them gunslingers' hands, find m' Appaloosa and settle the score. In that order! And I ain't f' arguin'!'

'Gold is in the mind. It has no beginning men can fathom, no future they can follow.' Tentrees eased his mount and Slocum's trailed horse to a walk and gestured for Heggerty to follow him into the shade of an overhang of rock. 'It is so,' he said dismounting.

'Apache thinkin',' said Heggerty. 'But mebbe yuh right.'

Tentrees patted the mount's neck and walked to the edge of the shade. 'Hawk Top is due north. Three hours. The woman, Crystal, and her party will be bringing wagons. They will hold to the easier desert trail. We shall move into the hills. In two hours, we shall see the party.'

Heggerty joined the Indian and gazed over the still, empty desert. 'And then?' he asked.

'You decide.'

Heggerty nodded. 'No way of knowin' where Stone's holed up with Miss Joni. Figure the Crystal woman is the only one who does know. Then there's Tranter...'

'No posse,' said Tentrees. 'Like you say, it should be close by now. Tranter has not left Bliss. More important to him that he should meet up with Slocum.'

'He's in f' a shock!'

'What will he do when he finds a dead man?'

'He sure won't be in no mood f' sittin' about mournin'!' grinned Heggerty.

Tentrees turned back to the mounts. 'Time to ride. We rest again in one hour.'

Heggerty rode easy, content now to leave the trailing to the Indian. His thoughts twisted through the maze of events since the bush-whacking, but he was not sorry to be rid for the moment of Logan. The man's only concerns were the gold and avenging the death of his son. He could hardly blame him, save that he carried his thoughts as bold as his guns. Only trouble with an obsession, Heggerty reflected, was that it left scant space for anything else.

Tentrees trailed steadily, directly north. The country changed from screes and rough scrub to the harder going of rocks and boulders, with the endless baked plain of white desert sprawling to a distant western horizon.

The riders passed into and out of shadows, their only sounds being the creak of tack, clip and occasional slither of hooves. There seemed to Heggerty to be no visible track for Tentrees to follow, but the Indian did not pause or falter until, emerging from the darker depths of a gulch to face a valley of outcrops that reached to high mountains, he reined up and pointed ahead.

'Old country,' he said as Heggerty drew level.

'Apache land?' asked Heggerty.

'For some. They know we are here.'

Heggerty looked anxiously round him. 'They watchin' us?'

'Watchin'. Waitin'.'

'Waitin' f' what?'

'Who can say?'

Heggerty eyed the Indian carefully, but stayed silent. If anyone could say, Tentrees could. 'Ceptin' that he won't! he murmured to his thoughts. Maybe it was as well.

Tentrees turned to him and smiled. 'Apache curiosity!'

But somehow Heggerty doubted it.

In another hour they had trailed the rim of the valley and moved into the thicker spread of rocks flanking the desert. Tentrees led the mounts into shelter and dismounted. 'Now we must wait,' he said, settling to watch the shimmer of space.

Heggerty tethered the horses and squatted at the Indian's side. 'Reckon they're close?' he asked.

Tentrees scooped a handful of sand and let it trickle through his fingers. 'When this is gone,' he said, his eyes still on the faceless space.

The first sign of the wagons' approach came in the distant swirl of a sand cloud to the south. Tentrees watched it closely, his empty fingers flexing lightly. Heggerty stiffened and came slowly to his feet.

'Time I was movin',' he murmured, turning to his mount.

'Ride with the sun at your back,' said the Indian.

Heggerty grunted and mounted. 'Stay close. I may need you.'

He walked his horse into the glare, his shadow long and hard at his side. The heat of the sun burned into his neck raising a lather of sweat. His eyes probed the sand cloud for shapes, noting every yard of its progress as it came on like a rolling mist of grey breath. How long, he wondered, before the outriders spotted him?

Suddenly, as if blown away on a ghost breeze, the cloud was still, dispersing, sand settling through the searing heat to leave the dark bulks of men, horses and wagons stark in the bright light. Two wagons, half-a-dozen men, maybe more, reckoned Heggerty, as he reined his mount to a halt and narrowed his stare on the group.

Seconds ticked by as the outriders watched him, wondering who he was, where he had come from—where he was heading.

Heggerty sat tight, flicked flies from his face, felt the sweat trickle down his back, soaking his shirt. He blinked as two riders separated from the group and rode towards him.

He recognized them long before they were close—the two who had met Slocum at the cave. The heavier man carried a Winchester; his leaner, fidgety partner already had a hand on the butt of his Colt. They rode on to within a few yards of him, reined up and stared hard.

The heavy man spat into the sand. 'Yuh lookin' f' somethin', mister?'

'Fresh coffee mebbe,' murmured Heggerty, his gaze moving between the two men.

'Yuh sure yuh ain't lookin' f' us?' asked the fidget.

'No, but I'm sure as hell glad t' see yuh. Lost m' trail back there t' the east. Figured I'd hit Apache country. Felt a mite lonely!'

87

Heggerty smiled thinly.

The heavy man spat again. 'Yuh gotta name?'

'Name's Heggerty. Y'selves?'

'Don't matter none.'

'Where yuh from?' asked the fidget.

'Eastways.'

'Headin' f' where?'

Heggerty shrugged. 'Sorta westwards.'

The fidget wiped the sweat from his face. 'Yuh a mite vague, mister. Too vague f' m' likin'.' The hand on the Colt butt had tightened, the first glint of metal flashed on the light as the man went for the draw—too late as he stared into the levelled barrel of Heggerty's gun.

'Easy, son. Easy,' grinned Heggerty.

The heavy man's mount side bucked and tossed its head. 'Hold it,' said the rider, a broad smile breaking his wet, gleaming face, the Winchester's barrel held high. 'If the man wants coffee, mebbe we can oblige.'

Heggerty holstered his Colt and grunted, but now his attention had passed from the men to the figure beyond them.

A tall, red-haired woman, a bull-whip in her right hand. He could already hear its slow crack as she flicked its tip into sand.

EIGHT

The woman's tallness was accentuated by her slim figure: long legs in tight, hugging pants and boots, a trim waist, firm breasts beneath her clean-cut shirt, elegant neck. Her hair, spread loosely across her shoulders, was a deep flame red, gleaming now like polished copper in the sunlight, but it was her eyes, a haunting, almost eerie green in the classically proportioned face, that held and devoured Heggerty's stare. One flash of them, he reckoned and a man might be driven to almost anything.

'Says he lost his trail back there in Apache country, Miss Crystal,' said the heavy man, his Winchester trained on Heggerty's back. 'Name's Heggerty. Hails from somewheres east.'

The woman drew the whip slowly through the sand until the tip lay at her feet like a sleeping snake. She watched it for a moment, then lifted her eyes to Heggerty and smiled.

'Lucky for you we were passing, Mister Heggerty.'

'I'd reckon that, ma'am,' said Heggerty. 'Be obliged if I could ride with yuh till I pick up m' trail again.'

'And where might that be heading?' asked the woman.

'Oh, anywheres west, ma'am,' answered Heggerty. 'I ain't fussed.'

'You drifting?'

'Yuh could say that.'

The woman looked at the tip of the whip again, then furled it quickly through her hands. 'Fix up our guest, Cal,' she said to the heavy man. 'It's time we were moving.'

There was a flurry of activity among the other men and within minutes the wagons were moving. The woman, without another word to anyone, disappeared into the back of the leading outfit.

Heggerty rode at the side of the heavy man, the fidget shadowing him. 'Some woman,' he said through a thin grin.

'Steer clear,' snapped the man. 'She

treats her men like a rattler.'

The fidget giggled. 'Yuh can bet on that!'

Heggerty waited a moment then said, 'Where yuh headin'?'

'None of yuh business, mister. Just ride.'

Heggerty shrugged. 'Suit y'self,' he murmured, and fell silent.

There was no easing of the pace through the long, hot day. The wagons rolled steadily, monotonously on through the sand to the dark mass of mountains and rock country ahead. There was no further sight of the woman. The heavy man stayed close to Heggerty, watching him without any acknowledgement of Heggerty's grins; the fidget roved the line of riders and wagons, never content with one place for more than a few minutes. All that broke the silence were the sounds of horses, creak of wagons, grind of wheels and jangle of tack. It was as if no one dared to speak, thought Heggerty; as if whatever they were riding to obsessed them. Maybe that was the way with gold.

But Heggerty's mind was busy enough. Logan had been right about Crystal—a woman to be kept at arm's length, but there was no disputing that she was the boss of the outfit and doubtless the brains behind the original robbery. How she figured with Tranter, and he with her, was something else. Point was, the wagons were moving to a precise destination. He just prayed that Stone and Joni Maggs were a part of it. If not...

Heggerty had shivered at the chill of the sweat on his neck and scanned the distant hills anxiously for a sight of Tentrees. But that, he knew, was a forlorn hope. The Indian was there, sure enough, but no one would ever know. The same might be said of the watching Apaches.

There were long shadows thickening to evening dusk when the leading wagon finally left the desert trail and turned into the scrub and shale of the foothills to the mountain range.

'Where are we now?' asked Heggerty of the heavy man as they reined up and dismounted.

'Hawk Top a few miles on. This is as far as we go till sun-up. We'll trail t' the Top t'morrow.'

'Then where?'

The heavy man narrowed his gaze on Heggerty. 'Yuh ask a mighty lot of questions f' a drifter, Heggerty. Who cares? Yuh sure as hell don't! Go and see if yuh can make y'self useful.'

Heggerty grinned, shrugged and strolled away, his eyes brightening as they took in the mound of Hawk Top. Somewhere up there, he reckoned...

But his thoughts were broken at the sudden clatter of hooves as a rider emerged from the shadows and slithered his mount to a halt a few yards ahead. In the same moment the woman climbed from the back of her wagon.

'Lucky,' she smiled, waiting for the man to dismount. 'Didn't expect to see you this early. How's things?'

Billy 'Lucky' Dimond, the baby of the Stone gang; loud, wild and gun crazy, Logan had said. Heggerty settled a steady gaze on the youth. Coming up twenty, he thought; slim, sharp, with wide, anxious eyes in a face that still had a baby smoothness about it, but there was no mistaking the fall of the arms to the long-fingered hands. This boy could shoot fast, instinctively, and enjoy watching his speed outgun his opponent.

But there was a harder look in Billy's eyes as he faced the woman. 'There's a whole heap of Apaches crawlin' around in them hills. They're worryin' Emmett a deal. He don't like Indians.'

Crystal smiled again and laid a hand on the young man's shoulder. 'No need to worry,' she said, the smile flashing as she pushed the flow of red hair into the nape of her neck. 'They're harmless enough. Maybe just curious. There ain't been Apache trouble hereabouts for years.' The smile eased. 'Stone getting edgy or something?'

'Says he'd feel happier if we pulled away from the Top t'night. He wants t' make f' Carney.'

The woman's face was suddenly taut. 'No! Not till I say so. Emmett stays where he is. So do you and Cy. No messing. You go and tell him that, Lucky.'

It was at that moment, as the young gunslinger turned angrily from the woman to his mount, that his eyes settled on Heggerty and did not move.

Was there a glimmer of recognition? Had he come close enough to Heggerty on that night in the cottonwoods to fix his face in his memory? If Lucky Dimond did remember...and then it was too late, and Heggerty knew it.

'I know yuh from some place, mister?' said Dimond, his round eyes narrowing as he peered through the gloom.

Heggerty stayed silent, unmoving.

The young man swung round to the woman. 'Yuh know this fella?' he asked. 'Where'd yuh pick him up?'

'Joined us back there on the trail. Said he'd lost his way in the hills. Name's Heggerty.' The woman frowned and was already reaching into the back of the wagon for the bull-whip.

'Like hell he was lost!' mouthed Dimond, facing Heggerty again. 'I crossed him just recent. He's been trailin' yuh!'

Heggerty stiffened. The sweat trickled icily down his spine. The woman moved to Dimond's side, the bull-whip furled in her hands. A Colt gleamed in the gunslinger's grip.

'You still reckon on how you've been drifting?' The woman spat out the words as if clearing dust from her throat.

Heggerty's fingers flexed at his sides, but there was no chance now of easing them to his guns. He shrugged and grinned. 'Young fella must be mistaken, ma'am. Never set eyes on this territory before.'

The woman unfurled the whip and let its tip drop menacingly to the ground. Dimond's eyes had widened again, their whites shining.

'No mistakin',' he snapped. 'I seen yuh, mister. Yuh ain't here by chance.' He glanced quickly at the woman as if awaiting an order.

'Maybe you'd like to tell us, Mister Heggerty,' said Crystal as she cracked the whip.

Heggerty backed, at the same time

slipping a hand to a Colt. His fingers had barely brushed the butt when the tip of the whip scorched his flesh like a hot poker. He backed again, hugging the torn hand to him.

'Well,' murmured the woman, moving a step closer, 'Are we going to hear from you?'

Heggerty was conscious of the other men gathering round him, the heavy one cradling his Winchester, the fidget shifting impatiently from one foot to the other, his sickly smile fixed on his wet lips. Dimond watched without blinking. The woman's green eyes were almost emerald in the fading light.

The whip cracked again, twisting itself round Heggerty's ankle, throwing him to the ground. Another crack, this time lashing mercilessly across his shoulders, ripping his shirt, stinging deep into flesh. Heggerty rolled, tried to come to his feet, but not before a third whiplash had scorched across his back. He lay still, wincing, trying desperately to blink sweat from his eyes.

He came slowly to his knees, half-turned to see the woman approaching, step by measured step, the whip flicking, writhing at her side like a black tentacle. He murmured a curse and slid back to his stomach in agony as the whip seared into flesh yet again.

'Let me finish him, Crystal,' snarled Dimond.

'No,' said the woman, standing over Heggerty. 'If the Apaches want something to keep them occupied, we'll give it to them. Bury him—up to his neck!'

NINE

Heggerty's eyes opened like heavy drapes being parted on a slow, uncertain light. He saw sand, miles of it; could taste it, was breathing it, and realized when he tried to move that he was cocooned in it. His face and head burned under the fierce morning sun, but his body was cold in its desert prison. His limbs were dead, immobile, and only his toes flexed in the depths of his boots. They might have been worms squirming against the sand grains.

He blinked, once, twice, until the far distance of the sand-scape came into focus. There was no sight of the wagons, but their wheel tracks heading into the mountain range were clear enough. The party had pulled out at first light.

'Sonofabitch!' he mouthed, and ran his tongue over his cracked, blistering lips. Come noon and those same lips would be as brittle as split rock. He struggled to shift—no chance, he was buried upright to the tip of his chin and bound hand and foot. Efficient! If the sun did not finish him, the Apaches would leave nothing worth picking over.

He closed his eyes, welcoming the darkness against the glare, and listened to the silence.

It might have been an hour later, maybe longer, when Heggerty's consciousness stirred from its dazed images of faces and places and he blinked again on the shimmer of desert—but this time there were sounds within it, far away, somewhere behind him. A dull, steady thud. Horses, riders, moving closer. Hell, if only he could turn his head! He heard a snort. The thudding stopped, came on again, this time slower. Voices. Words he did not understand.

Apache!

The sweat on Heggerty's face broke to a streaming lather, at first hot and burning, then colder until he was blinking on trickles of ice. The riders were closer, but now there was the faint sound of tack.

101

One rider with a saddle, thought Heggerty. How many others? He concentrated his hearing. Four. Five. A scouting party? Would they take him or finish him where he was?

He felt the ground shudder. Shadows grew around him, merged to a darkness that thickened as if some rogue cloud had drifted through the clear blue sky. And then silence again.

A horse pawed sand. Another snorted. The rider in the saddle slid to the ground. Heggerty's eyes stayed closed. He had no fancy to see what was coming. He just prayed it would be quick.

A hand settled on his head, ruffled his hair, wiped away the sweat. Heggerty's eyes opened to flickering slits. He peered into smooth dark features, a soft smile, and groaned.

He was staring into the face of Tentrees.

The heat-haze of the high noon had cleared on the touch of a gentle breeze when Heggerty finally stirred in the shade of the rocks and joined Tentrees where he sat watching the trail to the mountain range.

'Thanks,' he said, laying an arm across the Indian's shoulders. 'That was close. Too close. Your friends moved on?'

'We think we know where Miss Joni is being held. There is an old miner's hut at the foot of Hawk Top. My friends will watch till we are ready.'

Heggerty stiffened and narrowed his gaze on the glinting rock faces and smooth peak of Hawk Top to the North. 'Lucky f' you yuh found yuh friends,' he murmured.

'They found me,' smiled Tentrees. 'We came across you as we trailed back from the hills.'

Heggerty grunted. 'What about the wagons? We got any hint of their trail?'

'Lower reaches of the Top. Only trail for wagons. They will make the easier country again come sundown. We will be watching, do not fear.'

'We movin' now?'

Tentrees scooped a handful of pebbles. 'Soon, when the shadows are deeper. Then we move.'

Heggerty grunted again and went quietly

back to the shade. There was no point in arguing with the Indian; nothing to be gained through a show of impatience to be making for the hut—to Joni Maggs and the scum holding her. Better to wait, clean his Colts free of sand and listen to the trickle of pebbles.

Heggerty was dozing in the heady mix of heat and inactivity when Tentrees touched his shoulder.

'Now we move,' he said softly.

The shafts of the long shadows from Hawk Top had grown deeper and darker, so that Heggerty and Tentrees rode slowly into what might have been a gathering nightfall. The peak of the Top rose above them like the sprawl of a giant forehead below which, where the sunlight still glimmered on sharper outcrops, there seemed to be eyes, piercing and narrowed, watching them, unblinking and waiting.

Heggerty felt the sudden coolness of the shadows turn the sweat in his neck to a sticky chill. If there was ever a country that was haunted, where the spirits of old deaths and long dying still moved, this was it. Even the echoes, he reckoned, were dry-bone scared.

Tentrees rode easy and steadily north, hugging the depths of the shadows on a vague, one-horse trail that twisted and turned through boulders, narrow creeks and sudden gulches. He stayed silent, but his eyes were never still as they scanned to left and right and then into the rocky distance. Whatever his past in the Maggs' homestead, however long he had been there living in the style of the white man, he had lost nothing of his Apache instincts, thought Heggerty. And at this moment, he reckoned, gold was far from his thinking. He had a single objective: Joni Maggs. There was nothing else.

They had trailed for close on an hour when Tentrees reined up and indicated the twist of a broader trail below them.

'It was there,' he said, as Heggerty drew alongside him. 'That is where they raided the gold shipment. There was much slaughter that day.'

Heggerty stared at the spot—a bleak, empty place, shadow-filled and silent.

'Your people see anythin' of it?' he asked.

Tentrees turned his gaze slowly on Heggerty. 'They saw,' he murmured, and swung his mount back to the track.

But who and what had they seen, wondered Heggerty: faces they might still recognize? Had Crystal been with the raiders that day, or maybe close by, watching, smiling? The thought of the woman made him wince. The bull-whip burns still scorched. That was another score to be settled.

They trailed higher until the first sheer rock-faces of Hawk Top were like reaches of smooth grey skin at their sides, in one moment surrounding them, in the next parting to reveal unexpected spaces through which Heggerty could see clear to the spread of the northern plains.

But still no sight or sound of Apaches. Still nothing of the wagons or the hut. Only the silence and the haunting echoes of hooves on rocks, snorts on thin air and, closing like a curtain, the fading light as the sun eased away to the west. If there was nothing soon...

Tentrees raised an arm, halted and slid from his mount. He gestured for Heggerty to join him and pointed to the fierce glow of light trapped in the crease of a gulch. 'There,' he said.

Heggerty squatted and narrowed his eyes on the ramshackle heap of huddled stone and broken timbers of the miner's hut; a place long since abandoned and left to rot, until Stone had found it. The light came from a lantern glow in the small window to the right of the door. There was only one mount hitched at the rear.

'Mebbe we're a mite late,' murmured Heggerty. 'But that's Billy Dimond's horse. Recognize it from back there at the wagons. Yuh reckon the others have moved?'

'Maybe this Billy Dimond will tell us,' said Tentrees through a soft, slow grin.

Heggerty nodded. 'Mebbe. Yuh look t' the mounts. I'm goin' down there.'

'I will follow.'

They exchanged a quick, understanding glance as Heggerty moved to the thicker cover of rocks. He weaved smoothly, silently away from a direct approach to the front of the hut. His bet was that Billy Dimond would not be expecting visitors. The mystery was why he was still here if Stone, Bennett and the girl had gone, and where had they ridden to? Heading for Carney?

He dismissed the thoughts, paused, waited and watched. No sounds or movements from the hut. He scanned the ridges of the higher rocks. No sign of Apaches. Were they watching? He looked to his left, to his right. No hint of Tentrees. He moved on, one hand already settling to the butt of a Colt, the sweat in his neck chilling at the prospect of facing the baby-face's fast gun.

But just how fast was Billy Dimond? And how lucky?

TEN

Now the shadows were longer, deeper, burying the hut to a vague shape in the darkness of the setting sun and the approach of dusk. The silence tightened. Heggerty listened to the lift and fall of his own breathing. His eyes narrowed. Dare he risk moving closer to the hut?

His hand closed on the butt of a Colt. He shifted a foot, disturbed a stone, listened to it roll away, waited. Silence—and then the slow, eerie bounce of another stone somewhere at his back that came to rest at the side of his boot. Tentrees? Not Tentrees, he decided with a sudden turn. No Apache would be that untidy.

Heggerty's twist was a split-second too late. Even as he raised the Colt, fingered the trigger, there was a spit of flame, a vicious crack. Billy Dimond's deadly aim sent the Colt spinning from Heggerty's grip. He fell back, his left hand scrambling madly for the twin gun. He felt a burning stab of pain in his spine as he thudded against rock, winced, and through watering eyes saw the shadowy outline of Dimond.

The young gunslinger came a step closer, his body loose and relaxed, his eyes wild, his smile mocking.

'Well, now, if it ain't the drifter!' he laughed. 'Yuh sure get around some, mister. How'd yuh heave y'self outa the sand back there? Don't bother. Save yuh breath. I ain't in no mood f' draggin' this out. But I saw yuh sneakin' through them rocks. I got keen eyes, yuh see. Keen, mister, real keen.' He eased back the hammer on his gun. 'Better make sure of yuh this time, eh? No messin'.'

Heggerty squirmed. Tentrees—*where was Tentrees?*

It was the snort of a mount, the clip of a hoof on rock high above Billy Dimond that drew the man's attention and gave Heggerty the seconds he needed to roll clear of the line of fire. He slid into a swirl of stones, dropped into a tangle of dead brush and crawled deep into the shadows of its cover.

Dimond's smile faded, his eyes grown in his head like dancing moons. He crouched, waited for a moment, then scurried into the tumble of rocks and boulders to his left.

'Hell!' mouthed Heggerty, watching the disappearing shape of Dimond as he made for the hut and, more likely, his mount.

Heggerty rolled clear of the brush, came to his feet and went into a slithering run down the slope towards the light in the window. He ran parallel with Dimond, ducked and halted at the burst of another shot, but now the aim was high and frantic. He slithered on. Dimond dashed across the splay of light and was within two yards of his mount when Heggerty rose from the rocks behind him like a blade of deeper darkness.

'Bushwhacker!' he called, his left hand hovering at the remaining Colt. 'Yuh facin' me or simply runnin'?'

Billy Dimond froze, fingers reaching for the hitched mount's rein. He turned carefully, a body in gentle slow motion as if wafted on a breeze. The moon eyes danced again, the wet lips slid to a long, slobbering smile, faded and set to a grimace.

'Guess I'm callin' yuh, drifter.'

'Name's Heggerty. Remember?'

'I do indeed. I do indeed.'

Dimond's right hand was on his gun in an instant. The draw was smooth, touched with velvet ease, softer and faster than a slip of light.

But not fast enough.

There was a splintering, echoing roar from Heggerty's Colt, a spurt of angry flame that ripped the darkness apart; a glow of hunger for revenge in his eyes—and then the toppling, gut-gripping form of a man diving into death.

Billy 'Lucky' Dimond had played his last gun hand. The luck, he knew, in that final, moon-eyed stare into Heggerty's face, had run out.

Heggerty stared at the body, the loose, lifeless arms, the stiffening fingers on hands that had been so fast with a gun, still so young, and the baby face that had never grown a stubble.

'Darn fool,' he murmured.

He turned sharply at the snort of mounts, muffled clip of hooves, and stared into Tentrees' bright, watchful eyes and the faces of the half-dozen Apaches flanking him. There was a moment's silence before the Indian slid to the ground, stepped over the body without so much as a glance at it, and handed Heggerty the Colt Dimond had shot from his hand.

'You may need it sometime,' said Tentrees.

Heggerty grunted and wiped the sweat from his brow. 'Thanks,' he said. 'Yuh can bet on it.'

The Indian grinned. 'My friends here have been watching. We are too late. Two men and Miss Joni left one hour ago.'

Heggerty groaned. 'Where?'

'Maybe Carney. They have skirted the wagons to the west. Two friends following. I have said we will join with them at Long Creek before midnight.'

'We will,' said Heggerty. 'Best take a

look in the hut first. Didn't get around t' askin' this critter why he was still here. Must've been a reason.'

The one-room hut was dry, dusty and long into decay. There was a table, two chairs, a low blanket-strewn bed, and the single lantern still burning brightly in the window.

Heggerty moved slowly round the room, touching and turning over the few remaining items left behind. Tentrees drew his attention to the collection of food and cooking utensils on the table. 'Enough for three, maybe four days,' he said. 'The young gun was here to wait.'

'For what?' asked Heggerty.

The Indian stared through the open door into the thickening night. 'Gold,' he said softly.

Heggerty paused and turned, a thoughtful frown creasing his forehead. 'Yuh know somethin', yuh could be right at that.'

'The wagons would not drive openly into Bliss loaded with gold.'

'So t' make things look natural, yuh have drop-off-points—here, Slocum's cave—and collect quietly at yuh leisure. Stagin' posts f' a gold shipment. And mebbe Tranter's job is t' make sure it all runs smooth.' Heggerty brought a fist down on the table. 'Simple! But I reckon that's the way of it.' He grinned. 'We seem t' have upset the plannin' a mite!'

'Seems so,' said Tentrees. He moved to the door. 'But there is still Miss Joni.'

'I ain't forgetting,' said Heggerty, dousing the lantern and following the Apache into the darkness.

He had been careful not to let Tentrees see the girl's torn underclothing he had found on the bed. It had seemed easier to cover it up. But not so easy to hide his anger, worse, his fears.

The Apaches led Heggerty and Tentrees quietly from the hut on a trail that could hardly be seen but which the Indians followed instinctively. The night sky was open, a scudding mass of cloud caught on a freshening wind that threatened rain. Moonlight slipped over rock faces. High peaks were suddenly stark and then lost in the depth of darkness. The riders moved like shadows, silently and without changing pace. And the night closed in—deeper still on Heggerty's maze of thoughts.

He had no regrets over the deaths of Slocum and Billy Dimond. Bushwhackers and gunslingers had no place in his figuring. But Tentrees was right, the real fears were for the fate of Joni Maggs. Hang the gold, he thought; Logan, Crystal, Tranter, the whole miserable outfit could take their own chances. It was Joni that mattered.

And when she was safe, what then, he pondered through a low grunt? Then he would find the Appaloosa—almost certainly in the hands of Emmett Stone—and ride clear of the territory. As far away from sand and rock as he could get. Maybe somewhere west.

There was already a drift of rain on the wind when the leading Apaches came to a halt and waved for Tentrees to join them. Heggerty waited, hunched to a cold slump on his mount, the rain nibbling at his cheek.

'There is a fire glow up ahead,' said the Indian, rejoining him. 'Stone is there. Sheltered below an overhang. Bennett is with him.'

'Miss Joni?'

'She is there also.'

'Let's go!' croaked Heggerty.

Tentrees laid a hand on Heggerty's arm. 'Soon. Better to wait for first light. We could lose them in the dark. We wait.'

The Apache's eyes were as fixed and bright as stones in a pool.

Heggerty sighed, swallowed deeply and nodded. 'Like yuh say, friend—we wait.'

ELEVEN

Emmett Stone had made a shrewd choice. The hide he had selected for the night beneath the sprawl of the overhang at the far end of Long Creek gave a clear view of the land to the south. No chance of missing an approaching rider. The rock face above the hide climbed sheer to a craggy ridge. Scree and scattered boulders fell to the faint trail below. And the route to Carney and the north-west led deep into a wilderness of gulches.

Holed up tight and neat and darn near impregnable, thought Heggerty, as he licked rainwater from his lips and narrowed his eyes once again on the fading flames of the fire fronting the overhang. He could pick out the silhouetted shapes of Stone and Bennett, the Appaloosa hitched among the mounts, but as for Joni Maggs... There was no sign.

'The light will come soon,' said Tentrees, sliding to Heggerty's side in the cover of boulders. 'They will not move until then.'

Heggerty turned his gaze on the Indian. Now the Apache's eyes were dark, unblinking, as if staring into some future to which only the rainfall was a curtain, parting slowly, inevitably.

They were eyes filled with killing.

The first flush of light came with an easing of the rain to a slow, scattered drizzle on the steady wind. It slipped over the slabs of dull grey skies in the east like a smear of paint, and for the first time in hours the distant peaks were sharp and stark.

Heggerty blinked, stirred from his doze and turned instantly to peer at the curl of smoke from the dead fire at the overhang. No hint of movement, no sound of voices. He turned again to Tentrees crouched in the boulders to his right. The Indian simply nodded to where, far below him, an Apache was moving slowly, silently, like a hunting insect towards the mouth of the overhang. Another moved equally slowly, pausing, watching, listening, some distance away. A third had already reached the high ridge behind the hide.

Surrounded, thought Heggerty. The next move was up to the gunslingers.

The tall, rangy man who walked from the inner darkness of the hide to the half-light of morning, stretched and yawned and scratched the back of his head, was Cy Bennett; a mite older now, thought Heggerty, than the face on the poster Logan had shown him. The man stretched again, raised his face to the soft swirls of drizzle as if washing his stubble on its freshness, looked round him and turned back to the darkness of the hide.

Heggerty's fingers drummed lightly on the butt of a Colt. A trickle of sweat broke in his neck. Joni—where in hell was Joni?

Tentrees had moved and indicated for Heggerty to follow him when the silence and emptiness of the morning was ripped apart by the crash and roar of a rifle shot from somewhere beyond the overhang.

'What the hell!' croaked Heggerty, and

dropped into cover again at the splintering crack of another shot. He saw Tentrees squirming deeper into the rocks, then raised his head slowly.

A third shot roared, its echo flattening on the grey ceiling of cloud. Rain swirled across Heggerty's eyes, blurred his vision, but not before he had seen the sprawled bodies of the Apaches below him and the spreadeagled shape of the Indian on the ridge falling through the light like a limp and lifeless bird.

'Stone, goddamit!' snarled Heggerty as he crawled after Tentrees. How in tarnation had he managed...? Another shot, the ricochet ringing eerily round the rock faces; a mocking, jeering laugh, and then the voice growling out its message.

'OK, Apache scum, yuh just hold it there wherever yuh are. One move, one head above them rocks, and I'll blow yuh brains t' the wind. Yuh got that? Yuh hear me?' Stone paused, fired another shot high into the air. 'Cy?' He called again. 'Cy—yuh move out now, slow as yuh like, and bring that slippery bitch with yuh.' He raised his voice again. 'Anybody out there try anythin' and the woman's dead. No foolin'.'

'He is up there to the left of the overhang,' murmured Tentrees as Heggerty crawled to his side.

'Must've slipped out in the night. Sonofabitch!'

But now their stares were concentrated on the slow, shuffling movements in the darkness of the overhang. Bennett held Joni Maggs in front of him, her body taut and tense, her legs fighting for a hold against the man's grip and the remorseless drag as he edged closer to the break into boulders beyond the hide.

'Hell!' hissed Heggerty, the sweat in his neck chilling to an icy trickle as he watched the anguish, fear and flashes of anger on Joni's bruised and dirt-smeared face. Her clothes—what was left of them—were no more than rags, her hair a tousled mess, flattening now under the drift of rain.

Did Stone and Bennett intend taking the girl with them, holding her hostage, or would they abandon her once clear of the overhang? Had she served her purpose, or had Bennett still not had his fill of her? Heggerty swallowed deeply and eased forward. Tentrees laid a restraining hand on his shoulder.

'Easy,' he murmured. 'They will kill her, make no mistake.'

'Me first, I reckon,' grunted Heggerty and crawled away.

He had no idea how to get closer to Bennett, or if there was the time. No way of knowing what Stone and Bennett had in mind or planned. All he could think of and see was the struggling shape of Joni Maggs, fighting for her life. If she had the guts, so had he. Charlie would have reckoned on that.

He crawled deeper into cover, descending to the slopes of scree and loose stones, half hoping that he might work a way round to the edge of the overhang. But it was not only Bennett he had to contend with. There was Stone—and all the cards were in his hand.

He halted and through a gap between boulders watched Bennett working his carefully measured way from the hide. Joni was still struggling, her bare feet slithering for a grip on the rain-soaked rock.

'Hold on, gal!' murmured Heggerty, and moved on.

The sudden snort and snarl of Stone's rifle was the break he needed. Maybe another Apache hugging the scree had moved, catching Stone's eyes; maybe Tentrees had shown himself; maybe Stone was getting jittery.

He cleared the boulder cover in one leap, skidded in a tumbling heap of arms and legs through the scree and was suddenly within reach of the lower lip of the overhang. He gripped, fought the ache in every muscle, cursed silently and heaved himself on to the the flat, wet surface of old rock.

It took only seconds. They could be his last.

Bennett swung round, a vicious snarl twisting his lips, pulled Joni tighter to him and levelled the Colt in his left hand at Heggerty. The shot skimmed over the rock like a lick of flame. Heggerty rolled until he was into the darkness of the overhang and struggling to come to his knees. He blinked away the rain-mist from his eyes and drew his twin Colts.

'Goddamn yuh, Bennett!' he cursed, reached his feet and took a step forward.

Bennett's gun roared again, but the aim was low and wide. Heggerty took another step. Now he could see clear into the face of Joni Maggs, the rain and sweat mingled in a glistening lather on her cheeks, her eyes lit with fear, anger, hate, her limbs writhing against Bennett's grip. She gasped and tried vainly to kick against Bennett's legs.

Heggerty fell back, his gaze searching wildly for a target he could fire at, but there was only the girl, her heaving body, her flashing eyes, the curtain of rain. And then another roar, a sudden stab of pain as Bennett's shot winged Heggerty's upper arm, the clatter of a Colt hitting the ground.

Bennett's frame loomed closer, larger, like a black spectre. Heggerty saw the gun levelled at him, Bennett's twisted grin, and now the slumped body of Joni Maggs, her stare fixed in disbelief on Heggerty as she waited to see him die.

TWELVE

It was as Joni Maggs collapsed, her legs no longer able to keep her upright, her head failing forward, arms hanging lifelessly, that Bennett's concentration was broken. In one moment he was clutching the girl to him, in the next letting her slip from his grip, but the Colt in his hand never wavered. He snarled again, his lips wet, his eyes gleaming.

Now all Bennett had to do was ease the trigger...

The roar of the shot when it came echoed round the chamber of the overhang like a maddened dog's howl. Heggerty's ears filled, his head throbbed, the smell of cordite stabbing at his nostrils, but through the curl of clearing smoke he could see Bennett's left arm flung back, high and outstretched in an aim that had flashed wildly wide. His eyes glazed in a stare of shock, then narrowed in the searing agony of sudden pain.

He began to topple, slowly, like a felled tree, his haunted gaze fixed on Heggerty as if seeking an answer. He hit the rock face-down, and it was only then, in the rain-splashed light smudged with smoke, that Heggerty saw the knife buried deep in Bennett's neck, and beyond him on the lip of the overhang ledge the still, silent shape of Tentrees.

It was a long half-minute before the Indian grunted his satisfaction then calmly retrieved and cleaned his knife.

Emmett Stone had disappeared, drifted away soundlessly and without trace into the sprawl of hills and rocks at the rear of the overhang—and taken the Appaloosa with him.

Heggerty mouthed a quiet curse and winced as Tentrees tightened the bandage on his arm. 'How's the girl?' he asked.

'Sleeping,' said Tentrees. 'She will feel better after resting.'

Heggerty grunted. 'And you?'

The Indian's gaze settled on Heggerty's face. 'Easier now,' he murmured.

'I owe you—again,' said Heggerty.

A faint grin flickered over Tentrees' lips. 'Perhaps. We have Miss Joni, that is important.' He finished the bandaging and turned to where the Apaches were loading the bodies of their dead companions on their mounts. 'My people are angry. There will be revenge for these deaths. It is their way. They will ride to Carney when the time is right.' He turned back to Heggerty. 'You too will ride, my friend. It is in your eyes.'

Heggerty grunted again. 'I'll ride. I ain't plannin' on lettin' Stone go free. But you must return to the homestead. Get the girl home where she belongs. You agree?'

Tentrees shrugged. 'I agree. It will be best.'

'Good. Give me time to saddle up and I'll be gone. No point in breakin' m' neck chasin' Stone. I know where he's headin'.'

'Watch out for him. And Tranter will be closing by now.'

'I'll leave him f' Logan.'

Tentrees squatted and collected a handful of pebbles. 'You know much of this Logan?' he asked.

'Enough,' said Heggerty. 'Leastways, I'm reckoning on it.'

'Maybe.' Tentrees rattled the pebbles. 'He has the long look.'

Heggerty frowned. 'And what's that? Apache figurin'?'

'He looks far back. Maybe farther than you can see.'

'He's a deal to look back on.'

Tentrees scattered the pebbles. 'More than you know.' He came to his feet. 'I must say my farewells to my friends.'

'Give them m' thanks, and m' apologies. Didn't want things like this.'

'They will know. Like you say, Apache figuring.'

Joni Maggs was awake, wrapped in an Apache blanket, seated by a fire in the cover of the overhang and sipping coffee by the time Heggerty was ready to ride. He came quietly to her side and squatted.

'How yuh feelin?' he asked carefully.

'Like a louse!' she said, brushing the tangle of yellow hair into her neck. The blue of her eyes had faded to a pale grey, and her skin, only days ago so fresh and vital, had turned sallow, tight and tense. 'Knew yuh'd be back,' she added lightly.

'Not for these reasons—' began Heggerty.

'Tentrees has told me. Some of it. I'm sorry about the Appaloosa. About the trouble...' She swallowed quickly. 'About Charlie. He didn't deserve that.'

'Was it Stone?' asked Heggerty.

The girl nodded. 'Scum!' she hissed, and looked away. 'Specially Bennett. Him worst of all.' She turned to Heggerty again. 'Tentrees killed him. That was right. And you killed that kid, young Billy, and Slocum. That leaves only Stone... Yuh goin' after him?'

Heggerty grunted. 'I'm ridin' to Carney.' He waited a moment. 'Them critters say anythin' about a fella name of Logan?'

'I heard the name mentioned. Somethin' about gold and him knowin' all about it.'

'Any others?'

'Sheriff Tranter and that whore—' She hesitated. 'The woman they call Crystal. I seen her in Bliss. She in all this?'

'Pretty deep.'

'That figures. Tried t' buy our place once. Charlie wouldn't sell. Told her t' go t' hell. She whipped him and left.'

Heggerty felt a trickle of cold sweat in his neck. 'Yuh take care now,' he said quietly, laying a hand on the girl's arm. 'Tentrees is takin' yuh home.'

'I'll see yuh again? Yuh'll come back to Bliss?'

'Count on it,' smiled Heggerty, and stood up.

Joni Maggs watched Heggerty leave the overhang, speak briefly to Tentrees, then mount up and turn to the hills. She shivered, not because she was cold or felt the chill of the still swirling drizzle of rain, not even in her memories of Bennett. Her shiver lay in the sudden fear that she might have seen the last of the tall stranger she knew only as Heggerty.

The drifting mists of light rain continued throughout the morning as Heggerty trailed north towards Carney. He followed a track that twisted and turned through the rocks and straggling heaps of boulders, sometimes climbing along the cheeks of sheer faces, at others dropping easily into hidden creeks, gulches and the jagged splits of slim ravines. A still empty and haunted country, he thought, where not even the hawks flew and only the echoes of his own progress hovered round him.

Emmett Stone had taken the same trail—there was no doubt of that, he reckoned, judging by the fresh hoofmarks left in the few stretches of mud and wet sand. He was close on two hours ahead and moving fast.

Heggerty's thoughts in those first miles slid back once again to the desert, Bliss, Logan, Charlie Maggs and Joni and, with a quickening of his pulse, to Stone and the woman with the bull-whip. Strangely, they hardly dwelt on the gold, of whose it was or how it would be moved. There was something about the shipment he could not figure. Something was wrong.

But there was nothing wrong with the suddenly instinctive feeling he had that he was being followed. There were eyes on his back, and he found that a deal more troublesome.

THIRTEEN

Another hundred yards and Heggerty had rounded his mount into a deeper reach of rock and boulders. He dismounted quickly and slid into a cleft overlooking the track he had been following. He waited, watching. There had been no sound, no sight of the rider trailing him, but Heggerty knew he was not mistaken. He had an inner sense, a feeling that scrambled in the gut, when inquisitive strangers were that close, especially in wild country.

A minute passed. His mount snorted fretfully, the fresher wind at these heights whined through fissures and crevices, the rain danced. Heggerty wiped the dampness from his face, blinked, then watched the lone rider move into view.

He rode easy, slowly, his sodden long coat clinging to him, his head turning patiently from left to right as he scanned the ground for signs of tracks. 'Tranter!' murmured Heggerty. The sheriff had wasted no time. He looked as if he had been riding most of the night, maybe wondering how it was that Slocum had been gunned down and doubtless reaching firm conclusions by the time he had made it to the miner's hut and found Billy Dimond's body.

He would know, sure as fate, that Heggerty was heading north. But had he figured why, and had he known all along that Logan had been in Bliss? One thing was for certain: Heggerty had been set up for the killing of Joe Pine. Joe had died at the hands of Stone and his sidekicks, and Tranter knew it.

A trickle of cold sweat mingled with the rain in Heggerty's neck. Tranter would have been happy to see Heggerty hang for Joe's killing. 'Sonofabitch!' he hissed. Heggerty shifted his stiffening limbs in the grip of the cleft and pondered his next move.

Sure, he could take Tranter from here without any trouble, but maybe that would be the wrong move. Stone would have enough difficulty explaining the loss of his men to Crystal. And if Tranter failed to show up at Carney...that could be the wind to scatter the gold for good! No, he figured, it would be smarter to let Tranter reach Carney, but not without him carrying a warning of what was following.

Heggerty smiled softly to himself. Maybe it would be fitting for Tranter to ride into Carney with the grey chill of a ghost cooling his tail...

Heggerty had worked his way on foot, leading his mount into the higher crags of the rocks by the time the lift of a miserable noon light had come and gone. Now the rain was settled to a steady drift from thickening skies through which the wind whined like a lost child.

He had stayed a regular 300 yards ahead of Tranter, pausing occasionally to check the sheriff's progress. No question of it, Tranter's plan was to reach Carney by nightfall. Once clear of the hills, with or without a sight of Heggerty, he would ride hard for the town. Time was fast approaching to start irritating him!

Heggerty drew his mount into the shelter of a dry rock-face, hitched it and scanned the roll of a ledge above him. It was well within climbing distance and topped with a scattering of larger boulders and loose stones, Almost tailored for what he had in mind.

He scaled the face quickly and rolled on to the flat, wet rim of the ledge. He had a clear view of the narrow track twisting aimlessly northwards below him. Minutes passed, empty time filled only with the swirls of the wind, the drip of rain from rock to rock.

Tranter came slowly along the trail, his pace as steady as ever, his concentration still tight. His mount snorted and tossed its head. The sheriff reined in to the cover of the rock-face, halted and relaxed, tipping rainwater from the brim of his hat, then searching through the damp stickiness of his clothes for his baccy and matches. Heggerty waited, watching now for the first hint of smoke, the moment when

Tranter would be lost in the satisfaction of inhaling.

The smoke rose and cut away on the wind. Heggerty's fingers drummed lightly on a stone, slowed and settled in a firmer grip around it. He counted out three long seconds, then eased the stone from its bed and watched it roll to the lip of the ledge.

It fell to the left and behind Tranter, bounced once and was lost, its clatter sending a singing echo over the trail. Tranter's mount bucked; the sheriff cursed, dropped his smoke and grabbed the reins. His eyes lifted to the ledge—to a sprawl of grey space and swirls of rain.

Tranter cursed again, steadied the mount, and made to move on, but had gone less than a yard when a rush of stones fell around the mount's feet like a shower of black hail. The horse pawed the air, threatening to unseat its rider. Tranter bellowed, the mount whinnied, snorted, bucked and kicked. 'Easy! Easy!' roared Tranter, and slowly, gently calmed the sweating animal until it stood wild-eyed and panting under his tight hold.

He waited a moment, glanced at the ledge, then eased forward, a sudden coldness stiffening his back.

Heggerty smiled quietly to himself and slid gently from the ledge. Nice going so far, he thought, as he led his mount from shelter and into the high mass of rocks.

It was another hour before Heggerty halted again, this time well ahead of Tranter where the track began to widen and peter out in the drift of open land to Carney. The sheriff's progress had been slower, as if expecting that at any moment a shadow might grow at his back, or loom faceless and menacing ahead of him. Sure, the fall of stones might have been a natural slide, a flash collapse in the rain. But it might just as easily have been made by a man. Apache or Heggerty? He had no way of knowing.

He came on, his mount stepping high, flanks twitching nervously, until he reached the last of the narrow gorges carrying the trail to clearer country. He paused. He was sweating. His throat was dry, his eyes watery with rain. Maybe it was all imagination. Maybe he was tired, too tired to think straight. Maybe he was seeing things, hearing things in a silence where only the wind moaned.

But he was making no mistakes when it came to the sudden snarl of a gunshot high above him. He reined up, grabbing the mount on a short rein, then eased his right hand to the butt of a Winchester in its scabbard. His fingers gripped the smooth, wet surface. His arm moved on the draw, and then froze as a second shot scattered a rock-face a few yards ahead of him.

'Who are yuh?' he called, his voice splintering. 'Where are yuh?' His eyes gleamed, narrowed, widened. The sweat on his brow oozed and glistened.

He heard a twisting croak of laughter, hollow and taunting. 'Who'd yuh think, Tranter?' rang the voice. 'Who'd yuh think I am?'

'F' Crissake!' groaned Tranter.

A third shot spiralled, whined, faded in the grey of cloud and rock peaks. 'Joe Pine,' called the voice. 'It's Joe Pine here,

Tranter. Yuh remember me?'

Tranter shivered. The mount snorted.

'Yuh never seen a ghost, Tranter? Yuh will. Yuh sure as hell will! Heggerty'll bring me t' yuh. He'll bring me...'

Tranter loosed the mount into action and gave the horse its head through the gorge. The mocking laughter followed, echoing and surrounding him until its sound lay on the rain like a sting and lurked in every shadow of the gathering gloom.

And soon rider and mount had disappeared into the darkness of their own dread.

FOURTEEN

Heggerty smiled, a long, slow, satisfied smile that creased his weather-tanned face and held even under the dull throb of pain in his shoulder. He was still watching the sprawl of land to the north a half-hour after Tranter had headed at a pace into the gathering murk of grey evening; still seeing the racing mount and its rider slumped low on its neck, the billowing long coat, scrawls of splashed mud and the bewildered glaze in Tranter's eyes.

He could imagine the sheriff riding into Carney and spilling out his story to an uncompromising Crystal and the unforgiving Stone. How would they react? With surprise, or with hate and a determination to put an end to Heggerty? And when, he wondered, would Logan get to hear?

The smile faded. Logan, he reckoned,

would have kept a low profile in Carney, intent only on the gold and his personal revenge. But there were other scores to be settled: with Stone, with the woman, and there was still the recovery of the Appaloosa to be resolved.

The sweat broke sharp and cold in Heggerty's neck. Time had come to move, to ride to Carney and slip into it like a shadow.

Heggerty rode easy out of the hills and their stiff black rocks. He listened with a measure of content to the jangle of tack, the mount's soft snorts and comfortable touch of hooves to earth. The swirls of rain had moved west on a wind that had stiffened and then, like a breath, sighed itself out. The sky had cleared to a scud of loose clouds; there was a smear of high light, the promise of a moon and a welcome freshness on the air.

Good enough to be alive, he reckoned, save that the glow of late lanterns in Carney threw a haze that seemed to mirror a fate. How come he had ever gotten himself into such a miserable confusion, and all because of his goddamn curiosity over a place called Bliss? And how come...?

But by then he had Carney in sight.

For a gold town, Carney had no shine, nothing that mirrored boom or prosperity, or even the prospect of it. It seemed to Heggerty as he closed on it through the long drift of plain, to cower at the foot of the hills, scared of being there, bleak and, for all the noise, lonely as a chained dog waiting for something to happen.

A collection of forlorn, wind and rain-whipped tents were scattered round the outskirts of the few wooden buildings and single mud-swamped street. The brightest lights shone in the windows and from beyond the batwing doors of the saloon—The Last Nugget—and in the glow of a nearby workshop and livery. The rest was no more than brooding bulks and shadows, broken only by the gleaming stares of rainwater pools and puddles. A nowhere place of broken dreams and drunken hope.

Heggerty reined his mount into the deepest of the shadows, paused a moment, then moved on slowly, his eyes missing nothing, ears primed for the slightest sound beyond the slip of hooves to mud and the jangle of voices and music from the bar.

He had reached the first of the pitched tents when the flap lifted and the barrel of a rifle stabbed the darkness like a wet finger.

Heggerty reined up sharply, one hand slipping to the butt of a Colt. The rifle barrel hovered, withdrew and the flap opened.

'Reckon that's just about far enough, mister,' said the grizzled, toothless old man who stepped into the mud.

'Evenin',' said Heggerty, relaxing. 'This place Carney?'

'As ever was,' said the man, stepping closer, his grey eyes twinkling. 'Who's askin'?'

'Name's Heggerty.'

The old man spat over the barrel and lowered it carefully. 'Never heard of yuh.' His eyes narrowed. 'Yuh a gold man?'

'Sort of,' said Heggerty.

'Forget it. Ain't none here worth the pickin'.'

Heggerty shrugged. 'I can wait.'

'Yuh manage a lifetime? That's what it'll take.'

'Mind if I step down?' asked Heggerty.

'Suit y'self. Yuh use a whiskey?'

'Could I just!'

The man spat again and gestured for Heggerty to follow him.

The interior of the tent was a jumble of the old man's essential belongings, his few treasures and maybe most of whatever had made up his long years of toil. Pots, pans, blankets, a heap of worn clothes and boots, tools, some papers, faded photographs and a Bible were strewn on a low bed. Two crates served as chairs, a third as a food and drink store and table.

The old man lit a lantern and turned his attention to measuring out fingers of whiskey into tin mugs.

'They call me Shiner in these parts,' he said, watching the liquid slip from the bottle. 'That's on account of the gleam that used t' be in m' eyes. Faded a mite with the years. But I was christened close on seventy years ago J. John Jefferson Spencer. Never did rightly know what the first J stood for. Yuh health, mister.' He handed Heggerty a mug and raised his own. 'Yuh don't look a gold man. No wide-eyed gleam of hope in yuh eyes. I can tell. Spot a gold man first off. Seen enough in m' time.' He gulped at the whiskey, his gaze still on Heggerty's face. 'No I reckon yuh f' a driftin' man. And smart with them guns, shouldn't wonder.'

Heggerty grinned. 'Could be,' he said softly.

'No *could* be about it, mister!' He sniffed and slapped his lips together in loud appreciation of the drink on his gums. His eyes narrowed to darker slits. 'Interestin' how this mud-heap of a town seems t' be attractin' all manner of new faces lately.' He watched Heggerty stiffen. 'Comin' in like flies t' green meat. Yuh find that interestin', mister?'

Heggerty grunted. 'Seems like I might've timed things about right.'

'I'd figure that,' said Shiner, finishing his drink and helping himself to another. 'Wagons and critters outa Bliss, a fancy-danglin' woman, Sheriff Tranter lookin' hound-dog sick, a mean-lookin' gun-slinger...'

'Josh Logan?' asked Heggerty.

The old man took a deep gulp of his whiskey. 'Him too. Yuh know him?'

'In passin'.'

'He's here. Just outa town. Keepin' low, like he's waitin'. And that set me t' figurin' havin' the time f' it, yuh understand—and I figured that mebbe there's a few old bones about t' start rattlin'. Gold bones, mister. Yuh follow me?'

Heggerty nodded, his stare steady.

'Thought yuh might. Yuh got the look.' He paused again to savour the whiskey. 'A gold shipment outa Carney, biggest ever, went missin' a whiles back. Caused one helluva stir. Never did find it. But I've always reckoned it never went far. Instinct, yuh know. I can smell gold. Yessir, it's close, I'll stake m' life on it. And somebody knows just where. Interestin', ain't it—all them strangers arrivin' in Carney. And then Logan. Him most of all. Lost his boy in that raid.'

'I heard,' said Heggerty.

'Yuh seem t' have heard plenty, mister. Mebbe yuh'd care t'get t' tellin' me, and then mebbe I can get t' tellin' y'self a few things, should yuh be interested. And I reckon yuh are.' Shiner's eyes came alight. 'Just f' example, where I'm figurin' that gold's holed up.'

Heggerty finished his drink slowly, laid his mug aside and began his story from its beginning—on that night of a bushwhacking in the cottonwoods.

FIFTEEN

The night was deeper, keener, with a full moon riding high and bright and the wind easing back to a gentle breeze, when Heggerty and Shiner left the tent and made their way through the shadows towards the glow of Carney's lights.

'That's some story,' Shiner had said as Heggerty concluded with his description of the trailing of Tranter. 'Yuh been busy, mister, and it don't look as if yuh finished yet. Yuh want m' thinkin' on it? I reckon yuh've been duped right through. Only good thing so far is yuh sure seem t' have cleaned out some of the scum!' He had spat defiantly. 'Yuh goin' f' Stone?'

Heggerty had merely grunted. He had been more interested in listening to the old man's thoughts on where the gold shipment might be hidden.

'I been around these parts more years

than I care t' think back on,' Shiner had begun. 'Know the country, every twist and turn of it—the old workings, shafts, where t' pan, where not t' pan. Never had no real luck, though. A handful of dust, a few nuggets, that's about it. But, like I say, I know the country, and that's worth a deal hereabouts. It's survival. Take that place where Logan's holed up, Cloud Drift. Know that well. A plumb worked-out heap of nothing, but just the measure f' stayin' outa sight and still close t' Carney. Guess Logan had figured that f' himself.

'And then there's Elbow Creek...' The old man had rubbed his chin thoughtfully. 'Apache land. Sacred place. No territory f' the likes of you and me. Nobody goes there, 'ceptin' by mistake and usually just the once, but if yuh were intent on hidin' gold yuh sure as hell couldn't pick a safer place. And that, mister, is where I figure the shipment is buried. Meantime, if it's the Appaloosa that's yuh first thought, I reckon I know where yuh might find her.'

Carney had no more to recommend it on

a closer look than it did at a distance. 'Not the sorta place a man'd want t' put down roots,' said Shiner, pausing in the shadows at the far end of the street. 'Gold keeps a fella here, and when he ain't scratchin' f' it, he's got the saloon, the drink and the whores. That's Carney. Fortunes made and lost, all dependin' on the luck.' He pointed to the livery. 'There's more stablin' at the back. That's where the wagons are pulled up and where I reckon yuh'll find yuh mare. The woman and her sidekicks are in the saloon. I figure they'll mebbe make a move come sun-up.'

Heggerty settled his gaze on the livery. It seemed quiet enough in the soft glow of its lanterns. He guessed the saloon was claiming more attention at this hour, but any thoughts he had of watching and waiting for the woman and Stone were quickly dismissed. His priority was to get to Logan and then ride on to Elbow Creek.

'I'll get m' mount and meet yuh on the other side of town,' said Shiner. 'And no arguin', mister. If yuh plannin' on headin' f' Cloud Drift and meetin' up with Logan, yuh goin' t' need m' eyes—and m' nose f' gold.'

Heggerty offered no protest. It was true, he needed Shiner's knowledge of the country and, not least, another gun at his side.

'Make it fast!' grinned the old man as he melted into the night.

Heggerty waited only seconds before crossing to the livery through the deepest of the shadows. He paused a moment to give a rolling drunk time to clear the saloon and squelch away through the mud, then moved on, working his way to the rear of the stabling. There were no sounds, save the sharp snorts of the hitched mounts, the laughter and voices from the saloon, the whine of the lonely dog.

He reached a patch of darkness at the side of the open entrance to the stables, paused again, his eyes narrowed, his fingers light on the butt of a Colt. He whistled softly, that same, slow sound that only the Appaloosa would respond to, if she was there...

She was there! No mistaking that snort, the stamp of a hoof, the pawing of loose straw.

Heggerty took a step forward—and into the prodding gleam of a levelled gun barrel. Now there was no mistaking the giggle, the sudden brightness of eyes in a wet, frenzied face.

The fidget—the gunhand riding with the wagons. Heggerty stiffened. His hand slid from the Colt, the sweat in his neck turned icily cold.

'Well, if it ain't the driftin' man!' hissed the fidget, tightening his aim. 'Yuh sure are one f' gettin' around!'

Heggerty's stare moved from the barrel to the fidget's eyes. The man had missed his chance. He had hesitated when he should have blazed lead. Now he was relishing his moment.

'Reckon the lady'll thank me f' finishin' the job,' grinned the fidget.

Heggerty smiled. 'Mebbe yuh'd earn y'self another handful of gold.'

It was the mention of gold that changed the look in the fidget's eyes. 'What yuh know about gold?' he mouthed.

'Enough.' Heggerty's smile broadened. 'Just hope yuh don't lose out on yuh share. Yuh thought about that?'

'What yuh mean?'

'Gold's got a nasty habit of gettin' a mite scarce come a share-out.'

A line of sweat broke on the man's brow, his gun hand tightened, but now he was curious, the lips were hard and there was no hint of a giggle.

'I seen it before,' added Heggerty.

The fidget came a step closer, moving out of the darkness as if cut from it. 'Yuh tellin' me somethin', mister?' he croaked, his voice suddenly dry and cracked. 'Who the hell are yuh, anyway?'

Heggerty let his smile fade slowly, at the same time pursing his lips in a repeat of the whistle to the mare. The fidget frowned, took another step. The barrel of the gun gleamed in the light like a blade. Heggerty watched it, tensing for the mare's response, willing her to understand.

The horse's whinny, followed by a snort and stamp of a hoof snapped on the night

156

air like the breaking of a bone. Heggerty's reaction was a vicious kick that sent the gun spinning from the fidget's hand and rolled his eyes in a stab of pain. He came on in a rapid lunge and lightning smash of fist to jaw that caught the man long before he regained his balance.

The fidget groaned, then hit the ground in a sprawled tangle of stunned limbs. Heggerty dusted his knuckles. 'Never keep a man waitin' at the end of a barrel,' he murmured, and strode into the livery.

The mare tossed her head and nuzzled into Heggerty's shoulder as he heaved the saddle on to her back. 'Nice goin', gal,' he whispered. 'Yuh sure had the measure of that critter! Easy, now. Easy.'

Heggerty was mounted and steadying the mare's excitement when he saw the gleam of the fidget's gun barrel once again. Now the man was on his knees, levelling his aim, his eyes filled with dazed hate. This time there would be no hesitation, no split-second of waiting—but his trigger finger had barely taken the strain as Heggerty's twin Colts roared over the night like haunted thunder.

The fidget stared as if watching a beckoning ghost, fired high and wild and fell slowly face-down in the wet earth.

'Darned fool!' said Heggerty, and urged the mare into the darkness.

'Yuh sure have a way of stirrin' up trouble!' called Shiner as he rode hard at Heggerty's side. 'Guess the town'll know yuh around by now. Heard the lick of them guns a mile off.'

'Just keepin' them clean!' smiled Heggerty.

The old man spat into the wind. 'Ain't arguin', mister.' He pointed ahead to the mass of hills and peaks gathered on the night like black sleeping bodies. 'Follow this trail f' an hour, then turn west,' he called again. 'Cloud Drift's at the far end of a creek. Dead men's country.'

Heggerty's eyes narrowed as he settled to the mare's smooth gallop. Somehow, with the mount safe in his hands, the prospect held no chill. He was thinking of Charlie Maggs, Joni and Tentrees, the homestead and the life the girl and the Apache would have to begin again.

But soon his thoughts had moved on to the score still to be settled with a killer called Stone.

SIXTEEN

The moon was still high and the night an endless curtain of darkness as Heggerty and Shiner put the lights of Carney behind them and rode deeper into the hill country.

The old man seemed to sniff out the trail, weaving through the shadows like some mountain lion, holding to a pace that never slackened, until they had cleared the foothills and turned to the narrow track that twisted between stiff rock faces. Only then did he speak.

'Cloud Drift used t' be a gold-workin' area till the disaster. Big explosion, shook the whole place stupid. Twenty, mebbe thirty men died. The rest cleared out. Reckoned the Drift was bad luck.' He spat. 'I'd bet on Logan bein' holed up in what's left of one of the shacks, or mebbe an old shaft. Safe place t' stay hidden! Not likely t' be disturbed, that's f' sure!'

'He been around Carney?' asked Heggerty.

'Just watchin'. He won't have missed much.'

It took close on another hour to reach the lip of the Drift. 'That's it,' announced Shiner. 'Don't look any better by daylight.'

Cloud Drift shelved steadily from the track to a bowl-shaped spread of dry rock, scree and stone through which a thin stream snaked its way to an outlet on the far side. The remains of the workings stood stark and black, like bones long forgotten after flesh. A cool breeze shifted through the place. Could be the sighs of ghosts, thought Heggerty, tipping the brim of his hat. A dead man's land for sure.

'We goin' in?' asked the old man.

'Don't see why not,' said Heggerty, and eased the mare forward.

The sounds of their descent pitched to long, hollow echoes as the mounts disturbed stones and the sinewy runs of pebbles. Heggerty left the mare to find her own footing; he was more concerned with scanning the leftover shacks and mouths of shafts for anything that might hint of Logan. But there was nothing; no sounds, no movements, no snort of a mount. Logan must have gone deep, he thought. Or maybe he was already watching.

'Somethin's wrong,' said Shiner suddenly, dragging his mount to a slithering halt. 'Either he ain't here, or he ain't movin'.'

Heggerty reined up, his eyes narrowing, his body tense.

'Figure he should've shown by now,' added Shiner. 'Try f' that shack. Only one with anythin' like a roof left standin'.'

Heggerty eased forward again, his gaze steady on the opening that had once held a door. He came to within a few feet of it, halted and dismounted then indicated for the old man to follow him.

A shimmer of moonlight clipped the skeleton of roof rafters, slid along the stone wall and faded under a scudding of cloud. Heggerty waited, listening, wondering why there was still no sound of Logan's mount. Maybe this was not his hideout. Maybe the old man had got it wrong...no, not wrong!

Too darned gruesomely *right!*

Heggerty stared down at the body sprawled within a few feet of the threshold. Logan lay face down, tied hand and foot, in a still sticky pool of his own blood. Most of the back of his head had been shot away, but it was his bare back, whipped so viciously that the flesh had been stripped away to leave the bones exposed, that held Heggerty's stare, churning his stomach and raising a twist of cold sweat in his neck. 'F' Crissake,' he murmured, and closed his eyes.

Shiner groaned at his side, turned away and spat into the stones. 'Who in tarnation—?' he began.

'The woman, the one they call Crystal,' said Heggerty.

'She knew Logan was here, knew where t' find him... Hell, mister, what sort of a woman is it...? She must be...'

'I know exactly what she is,' clipped Heggerty.

Shiner saw the sudden glow in Heggerty's eyes, a light that burned like a

163

dance of flame. 'What now?' he asked softly.

Heggerty blinked and grunted. 'We clear up here. This fella deserves a decent burial. Then we ride.' He lifted his gaze to the tips of the black peaks of Cloud Drift. 'We ride hard!'

First light had shown itself and lifted the heavy gloom of the Drift by the time Heggerty and Shiner had found a suitable resting place for Logan and covered the shallow grave with stones. The old man had constructed a rough wooden cross on which he had carved the simple epitaph: Marshal Josh Logan. 'Reckon he was always a lawman at heart,' he had said. 'Man don't change that much.'

Who had ever really known what was in Logan's heart, wondered Heggerty; hatred and revenge for the death of his boy? Or maybe within that hatred he had still been on the side of the law. Maybe he would have taken those responsible to the justice of a court—or maybe he would have shot them where they stood.

Heggerty grunted to himself. Whatever, Logan had not deserved to die as he had, and that, Heggerty reckoned, made everything as clear as the oncoming day. 'Saddle up, and let's move,' he called to Shiner, then took a last look at the grave and turned from it.

The old man gathered the mounts and, with his back to the now clearing peaks, said, 'Don't look too close, mister, but we got company. Apache skitterin' round in them hills like termites. Been there some time.'

Heggerty's eyes narrowed on the sweep of the range. 'Could be just curious,' he said.

The old man spat. 'Could be. On the other hand, mebbe not. Apaches ain't never *just curious*'.

Heggerty mounted up. 'We'll find out, won't we?'

It was a slow, meandering trail out of Cloud Drift deeper into the hills to the north and Elbow Creek. Shiner rode ahead, picking out the best of the track, leaving Heggerty to concentrate on the crawl of rocks and the following Apaches.

'No doubt about it,' the old man said, 'the Indians are goin' t' stay close. And I don't reckon they'll take kindly t' us passin' int' the Creek. Mebbe we should let the woman and her sidekicks get there first.'

Maybe, thought Heggerty, but there were other things occupying his mind. It seemed clear enough now that Crystal had planned on breaking up the shipment once she had it in her hands—with Dimond and Slocum and perhaps Tranter—for collection in smaller amounts later. She would have returned to Bliss with a barely noticeable wagonload. But what would she do now that the men at the staging posts were dead? Replace them, or switch tactics? How would Stone and Tranter react? Did they trust the woman? Did she trust them? Who dared their trust when gold was the prize?

He had grunted to himself and turned his thoughts to Tentrees and Joni Maggs. They would be back at the homestead by now, back to the new loneliness of

166

a home without Charlie. And then his thoughts had faded to let in the grisly images of Logan and that last sight of him as they had lowered his body to the shallow grave. Strange, he thought, that in that final moment Logan's face had lost its pain and agony. It had seemed almost peaceful; there might even have been a soft smile on the broken lips.

He shuddered. He was tired, hungry and cold in that first clamour of the new day. Maybe he had simply had enough, or maybe it was the prospect of Elbow Creek.

'Them Apaches still close?' asked Shiner as they topped the climb of the track.

'Close enough,' replied Heggerty. 'Six, mebbe eight, keepin' t' the eastern side.'

'It figures,' said the old man. 'East side of the Creek is sacred ground. They ain't goin' t' let us in there.'

Heggerty reined up alongside him. 'That where the gold is?'

'Don't reckon so. More likely t' the west. I'll show yuh.'

They rode on slowly, keeping to the

track as it turned and twisted through the boulders and giant outcrops, rounded rock faces and finally began to descend into the half-lit closeness of the Creek. The full light had not reached here in spite of the lifting day, but the shadows looked permanent as if the night had spilled its overflow and left it.

'Down there,' said Shiner a half-hour later, pointing to a sprawl of scree to a sheer face. 'There's any amount of caves, ideal f' hidin' a shipment. Trail lies just outa sight. Yuh could get a wagon t' within mebbe quarter-mile of there, then it's all heave and sweat.'

'That's where they'll be,' said Heggerty moving on.

'Not so fast, mister,' croaked the old man. 'Best take a longer look—t' yuh right, foot of that scree.'

Heggerty turned his gaze to the scree and the cold grey of the light covering it. He recognized the body of the man sprawled on the stones; recognized the Winchester at his side, and there was no mistaking the three arrows stiff and tight in

168

his back. One of Crystal's men, the heavy sidekick she had called Cal.

'Seems like I was right,' said Shiner, 'but a dam sight too late.' He spat and wiped his mouth. 'Ain't lookin' forward t' what we'll find down there, mister. And that's a fact!'

SEVENTEEN

'I'm crossin' t' the scree,' said Heggerty tightly. 'Cover me from here.' He dismounted and handed the reins of his mount to Shiner. 'And no arguin'!'

The old man spat again and grunted. 'Yuh got the wagons t' yuh left, Apaches t' yuh right—mangy odds, mister, real mangy.'

'Yuh keep them Apaches occupied if they get too keen a likin' f' me. Yuh got it?'

'I got it. Yuh just watch out f' y'self OK?'

Heggerty nodded, patted the mare's neck and slid away to where Shiner reckoned the wagons were drawn up.

The old man was right, he thought as he scrambled over the rocks, the odds were mangy, but Stone and the woman were here, somewhere, and the images of

Logan had not faded. Hang the gold—this was all about the deaths of good men—Joe Pine, Charlie Maggs and the marshal—and the sickening abuse of a young woman, a bushwhacking and a long walk through the desert. Too much for one man to stomach and think only of the odds against him. They would have to stay mangy.

Heggerty descended deeper into the Creek through a cleft between high reaches of rock. The two wagons were drawn together well ahead of him at the start of the scree slope where the trail petered out. He counted six, seven, eight men in cover beneath them, their rifles trained blindly on the surrounding peaks at an enemy they could not see. He spotted Tranter deep in the shadow of the leading wagon, but there was no sign of Stone and the woman.

'Goddamit!' he mouthed, and shifted his gaze back to the grey slopes of the scree.

Supposing Crystal, Stone and the side-kick, Cal, had set off for one of the caves in the rocks. Cal had not made it, but maybe the others had, and maybe they were up there now, pawing over the gold. Heggerty's eyes narrowed on the jagged claws of the high-reaching rock-faces and their stark black peaks. Somewhere up there, he reckoned.

He moved on, skirting the rear of the wagons through the rock cover. He could not risk crossing open ground, but if he could work his way in a half-circle to the caves... It would take time and he was already sticky in the flat, heavy air of the morning. The sweat in his neck was hot. He would feel a deal easier at the first touch of its chill.

It took only minutes, but it seemed like an hour, for Heggerty to reach the rocks above the scree. He rested in cover, wiped the sweat from his face and let his gaze range over the scene. No sign of the Apaches or Shiner, no movement at the wagons, save for the occasional nervous twitch of limbs as Tranter and his men waited to come under attack, but more importantly neither sight nor sound of Stone and the woman. He reckoned he was right. They had made

172

it to a cave somewhere close to where Cal lay dead. Question was, which cave?

A sudden flash of rifle fire at the wagons split the silence. The Apaches had moved in closer. Heggerty waited, five, ten seconds, then, as the firing subsided and the Apaches moved on in their taunting stalk, headed bent double for the scree, reached it and flung himself into the mouth of the nearest cave.

He blinked in the darkness, came to his feet and pressed his back to the cold rock of the cave wall. Nothing to see, nothing to hear. Maybe the wrong cave. He went deeper, paused, listened, blinked again, but now he could smell something...sweat, fresh, excited sweat on a man close by.

Stone! It had to be Stone.

Heggerty's fingers rested on the butt of his Colt. The sweat in his neck was colder, his eyes steady. A match flared ahead of him, a brief, bright burst of light that illuminated Stone's face for a moment and was just as instantly doused.

Heggerty moved softly to his left, his

173

breathing tight, his touch tensing on the gun. Would Stone risk a shot at a target he could only guess at? Now he could hear the rasp of the man's breath and still smell his sweat. Stone was in no hurry, but where was the woman?

'I'm told they call yuh Heggerty,' said the voice from the darkness. 'Never heard of yuh, but I sure ain't fixin' on havin' yuh around.'

Heggerty stayed silent, straining to pinpoint the sound.

'Yuh a friend of Logan's?' asked Stone.

Heggerty remained silent.

'Not anymore yuh ain't!' laughed Stone. There was the scuff of a boot over pebbles, the eerie click of a hammer primed on a Colt. 'He bought it rough,' said Stone. 'It'll be easier in your case. I ain't got the time f' entertainment.'

Heggerty had dropped to a crouch and moved deeper to his left. He still had his back to the cave wall, the ground at his feet was even and firm, but now his eyes were stinging with the strain of trying to pierce the darkness for shapes. Stone seemed to have stayed still; only the stiff smell of him lingered.

Time to take a chance, decided Heggerty.

He scuttled on, felt the first shelving of the cave floor and was flat on his stomach when Stone's Colt roared in a flash of flame. The shot went high, splintering the wall rock and ricocheting into the darkness. Heggerty's instinct was to return fire, but he waited, listening for the slightest sound of Stone moving.

Silence. Heggerty swallowed on a dry, parched throat. He blinked away sweat, felt a slow trickle of it down his neck. 'Move, darn yuh!' he mouthed on his breath.

Seconds passed, and then Stone shifted. He had turned and was moving deeper into the cave. Heggerty followed, scuttling blindly after the sound of footfalls, hugging the wall wherever he could feel it, conscious that at any moment the man might stop, turn again and let his Colt rip.

Silence again. Stone had stopped somewhere up ahead.

Heggerty paused, leaned on the cold

175

rock and squinted into the darkness. He took a deep breath, a firmer grip on his gun and went forward, one slow, careful step at a time. He felt the wall begin to curve to the right, the floor to climb. Was he being fooled, or was that the soft haze of light he could see?

He paused again, listened. Another step; two, three, four. Now he was rounding the bend. The light grew from a haze to a brighter glow that lit the cave walls. He was coming back to the daylight somewhere at the rear of the hill range. His steps quickened, then froze at the sudden sprawl of Stone's shadow across the cave floor.

Heggerty drew his second Colt, pushed himself clear of the wall and stood tall in the light, his guns blazing with a shattering, echoing roar at the shape of the man silhouetted in the sunlit gap at the end of the cave. The shots were rapid, spitting into the light like vicious tongues, too fast for Stone to react to, save to leap clear of the gap as if tossed aside in the grip of a whirlwind.

He was on his knees in sand, hatless and

sweat-soaked when Heggerty appeared in the full glare of the light at the gap.

'Sonofabitch!' groaned Stone, His greasy lips curled in a snarl.

'On yuh feet,' snapped Heggerty, thrusting his Colts forward. 'On yuh feet and start walkin'.'

Stone came slowly upright, his eyes filled with a glaring hate. He reached for his hat, but too late as Heggerty's gunshot lifted it clear of him.

'Yuh won't be needin' that,' said Heggerty. 'Now walk, bushwhacker!'

Stone frowned in a moment of vague recollection as if seeing some shimmer of a ghost from a long past.

'Walk!'

The man turned, stumbled, regained his balance and took his first slow steps through the scorching sand.

Heggerty waited, tensed but steady, the sweat cool in his neck, his eyes narrowed on Stone's back. It would take the man just six steps to make his decision... Three, four. Six steps before he risked the final gamble and played his card as a gunslinger.

Five... The only card he had ever held. Six...

Stone swung round, a gun tight in his hand, his stare glassy, a drool of spittle at the corner of his mouth, but even as his trigger finger settled he heard the roar of Heggerty's Colts and felt the sudden, thrusting violence of the burning in his chest. He was flung high in a whirl of arms and legs, fell back with a thud and was still, his stare fixed, the spittle trickling softly into sand.

'Go down, Emmett Stone, down t' yuh hell!' grunted Heggerty. He holstered his guns and had taken a step away from the gap when the bull-whip cracked, wrapped itself round his leg and dragged him to the ground.

The woman's laughter rose on the air like the screech of a hunting hawk at her kill.

EIGHTEEN

'Nice shooting, mister. Smooth as my butt! But not smart enough.' Crystal tightened the hold of the whip on Heggerty's leg and walked slowly towards him. She smiled, tossed her red hair over her shoulders and flashed her green eyes in a glare of triumph. 'He had that coming,' she said, glancing at Stone's body. 'Last of the bad bastards!' She reached Heggerty and looked down at him. 'Wouldn't take you a second to draw one of them fancy Colts and finish me now.' Her tongue rolled seductively over her lips. 'Or maybe I've been figuring you all wrong. Maybe you've lost your nerve.'

Heggerty wiped sand from his face, pulled down the brim of his hat to shade his eyes and propped himself up on his elbows. 'No ma'am,' he said gently, 'Yuh been figurin' me dead right, but I ain't never had cause t' shoot a woman. Not yet.'

The woman's smile broadened as she relaxed and took her weight on one hip above the long reach of legs. 'Took a liking to you the minute I set eyes on you, Heggerty. You're my kind of man.'

Heggerty returned the smile. 'That why yuh buried me neck-deep back there?'

'Just playing!' laughed Crystal.

'Too rough f' me ma'am.' Heggerty unwound the whip from his leg and tossed it aside. 'Yuh were playin' with Logan too?' His eyes narrowed in a cold stare.

'He asked for it. I don't suffer fools.'

'Seems so,' said Heggerty. 'Gold can get t' yuh like that.'

The woman watched him for a moment, her gaze probing and questioning. She furled the whip and let it hang loosely at her side. 'Maybe we should talk about that.'

'Mebbe we should, ma'am.'

'I don't know how you got involved in all this, mister, but you sure as hell seem to have gotten deep. I heard what you did to Stone's men, and I heard...'

A shuddering roar of rifle fire from the other side of the hill range brought Heggerty to his feet. 'Seems like yuh friend Tranter's got Apache trouble.' He glanced at the woman whose expression had changed instantly at the first crack of shots. Now the eyes were duller, as if staring into some private dread, the lips tighter, the body stiff. She shivered at the pitched echo of a scream. 'Real trouble,' murmured Heggerty as he turned to move back to the cave.

'No, wait! croaked Crystal, gripping Heggerty's arm. 'Listen to me.'

'Yuh'd best make it fast, ma'am.'

'There isn't any gold,' she said, her voice suddenly unsteady. 'Leastways, not here, not where it should be.'

Heggerty felt a new surge of sweat in his neck.

'Sure, I organized the raid on the shipment,' the woman went on. 'It was all my doing, my planning. The haul was too big to handle in one go, so it was hidden here, in that cave. This is safe territory,

Apache burial ground, and I figured no one would come looking for it. Plan was to leave it awhile, then ship it out to drop-off points, make a share-out to Stone and his men and Tranter, and then I'd be gone—somewhere's East.' She paused tightening her grip on the whip. 'But there isn't any gold. Somebody's taken it.'

'Yuh men killed Logan's boy?' murmured Heggerty without moving.

'I didn't know he was outriding with the shipment, not till later.'

'Too late f' him and the others.'

The woman's eyes flashed. 'You sitting in judgement, mister?'

'On yuh conscience, ma'am.'

She backed and tossed her hair again. 'Maybe you know where the gold is? Maybe Logan told you?'

'Yuh reckon he took it?' asked Heggerty.

'He didn't say.'

Heggerty's eyes narrowed to dark slits. 'But yuh sure figured he'd never get t' it if he had.'

'He was in the way, a nosey danger. I just wanted to know how much he knew.

I didn't know then the gold wasn't here. And, in any case, he knew too much.'

'Yuh sure one helluva bitch!' said Heggerty deeply. 'And right now—'

'Don't be a fool, Heggerty. Help me find the shipment and a half of it's yours. That's a deal.'

The sweat in Heggerty's neck had turned to a cold trickle. 'Sure,' he said slowly. 'A real deal, about as fair as yuh gave Logan and Charlie Maggs!' And then he turned to the cave.

The whip cracked again, slashing across Heggerty's back like a lick of flame. 'Bitch!' he mouthed as he fell face-down into sand. Another crack, this time ripping into his shoulder. He rolled over, his fingers scrambling for the butt of a Colt. He had never shot a woman, but now...

He blinked. She had gone!

Heggerty squinted into the glare of the sun, to the shimmering, shadowy rise of the hills. She was there, already working her way higher, moving through the rocks like an excited lizard seeking the heat.

'Bitch!' he mouthed again, and lunged after her.

She climbed quickly, her limbs lithe and supple as she hauled herself from rock to rock. She looked back only once to see Heggerty following on the same route, his face fierce with anger.

The shooting beyond the hill peaks continued. Tranter and his men were standing their ground, thought Heggerty. But for how long? They would be no match for the Apaches in the long run. The Indians would simply wear them down, picking off their targets one by one.

Heggerty paused. The woman was still well ahead of him, but where was she heading and to what end? Did she plan on teaming up with Tranter again? But if she fell into Apache hands...she would have no illusions about that fate.

The woman stopped, looked round her, down to where Heggerty climbed on, and then up on the higher reaches. It was a sheer drop to the scree from there.

'Goddammit!' cursed Heggerty as he grabbed the next hand-hold and heaved his worn body into another mound of rocks.

He climbed in and out of shadow, avoiding wherever possible the full glare of the sun, but conscious now of his shirt and pants clinging to him as the sweating increased; conscious too of the trickling blood from the bull-whip wounds.

He had gained on the woman when a movement far below him drew his attention. He halted and looked closer. Shiner! The old miner must have worked his way round from the other side of the Creek. Now, as he cradled a Winchester in his arms, he stared first at the body of Stone and then at the hills, shading his eyes against the sun's glare.

It took only seconds for him to spot the woman and return Heggerty's wave. Slowly, like a hunter taking his time to target on a grazing deer, he levelled the Winchester on the woman.

'No!' yelled Heggerty, the sound echoing over the troughs and folds of the hills. Shiner waited, holding the aim. 'No!' yelled Heggerty again. Shiner lowered the rifle and made for the foot of the rocks.

Heggerty sighed and climbed again, but now the woman had reached the peaks and was threading her way through them. Where in hell's name was she heading? Heggerty thrust his limbs into still greater effort, scrambling through the rocks as if driven by a madness.

He had come to within a few feet of the peak when a flurry of rifle fire from the floor of the Creek spluttered and whined round the woman like a swarm of crazed bees. The Apaches had seen her!

He watched her stumble, regain her feet, stand tall, still clutching the whip, her breasts thrust into the brilliant light, her hair dancing gently on the faint breeze. She spun round to face Heggerty, smiled, threw back her head in laughter and then plummeted out of his sight, down to the sun-streaked scree.

Heggerty squirmed on and lay flat on his stomach to gaze into the Creek below him. Crystal's body lay like a twist of driftwood on the stones, her red hair massed round her head, the staring green eyes catching the sunlight. The bull-whip was still in her hand, unfurled, snaking darkly into the blood that oozed from her side. It was hard to tell from her broken lips if she had died with a grimace or a smile.

Maybe it hardly mattered now, thought Heggerty.

NINETEEN

The sun was fierce and fixed like an eye in the clear blue sky as Heggerty and Shiner crunched their way over rocks to the tumble of the scree. A sad, almost sullen silence had descended over Elbow Creek; the gunfire had ceased, the dead lay where they had fallen, the living waited in the shadows. Far to the south a hawk drifted soundlessly, alone and watching.

'Nothin' t' be said f' a bitch like that,' said Shiner, spitting over his shoulder. 'Good lookers come and go—they all die the same.' He spat again. 'Say this f' her, though, she sure made a real job of it, fallin' like that under them bullets. Style, mister. She had style. A bitch of the best!'

Heggerty grunted, winced as he shrugged his shoulders beneath the cling of his shirt, and halted to gaze over the sprawl of the sun-baked Creek. There was no movement at the wagons. A group of mounted Apaches waited, watching in the shade of the rock overhang.

'Seems like things have quietened down,' he murmured.

Shiner shouldered his rifle and squatted on a boulder. 'Two ways of lookin' at it, mister—either we're ghosts or them Apaches out there just happen t' be on our side.' He ran a hand over his eyes. 'I'd figure on them bein' with us. Yuh reckon?'

'I reckon,' said Heggerty.

'Which leaves me wonderin'—where in tarnation is all that gold we been fightin' over? Yuh tell me that, mister? Just tell me.'

'No idea,' said Heggerty, and crunched on to the scree.

It was true, he had no idea, nor in that moment was he much bothered. His thoughts were still in turmoil over the killing of Logan, the shooting of Stone and the death of the woman. Crystal had chosen her own way to her end, perhaps in the certain knowledge that without Heggerty's co-operation she had no hope of recovering the gold. But would he have shot her? He had been close to it, yet had stopped Shiner in his aim. There had been no doubt in the old man's mind. Maybe there had been none in his. Maybe he would have pulled the trigger. He would never know.

But as for the gold—that was something else. It had been moved, but to where, and who had moved it? The Apaches, raiders who had stumbled on it? Logan? He halted again and narrowed his eyes on the Indians. They had made no attempt to move from where they waited in the shade of the rocks. Looked as if their fighting was over for the day. Leastways, an old man and a weary drifter posed no problem to them. They were right!

'Never any accountin' f' Apaches,' mused Shiner. 'One minute skinnin' the hide off everthin' that moves, the next sittin' around doin' nothin'.'

Heggerty and Shiner crunched on in a direct line to the group until they were within a hundred yards of them, then slowed their pace as the Indians moved apart and one man stepped forward.

'Well I'll be—' began Heggerty as Tentrees came towards him. 'If it ain't—'

'This the fella yuh were tellin' me about?' asked Shiner.

'As ever was!' smiled Heggerty.

Tentrees grinned and held out a hand.

'How the devil—' began Heggerty again, taking Tentrees' grip. 'I thought...here, meet Shiner.'

The two men exchanged greetings. 'Never more pleased t' see yuh, and that's a fact,' said the old man.

'Joni—what about Joni?' said Heggerty.

'Safe at the homestead, waiting for us,' explained Tentrees. 'She agreed that I should return. We knew what was in your mind. Miss Joni said she would feel easier if you had help.' He gestured to the group. 'My friends have been watching.'

Heggerty grunted and mopped his brow.

'We have taken three men alive,' Tentrees went on calmly. 'One of them is Tranter. The others...they should not have been here. No one should be here.'

'Yuh right,' said Heggerty. 'Our apologies f' trespassin'.'

Tentrees nodded. 'We understand, but now we must leave.' He made a sign to the group who began to prepare to move out. 'My friends will help us on our way to the lands bordering Bliss. Then they will return to Cloud Drift. To guard the gold until it can be moved.'

'*Gold!*' spluttered Shiner. 'Yuh say gold? Yuh know where it is?'

'We know,' said Tentrees. 'It is at the hut where you found Logan. Beneath the floorboards. Logan had been moving it from the cave for many months, helped by my friends.'

'Bless m'crumblin' bones!' spat Shiner.

Heggerty sighed. 'So he knew all along. It was there, right where they killed him. All he wanted was—'

'Justice—with your help,' said Tentrees.

Heggerty turned his gaze to the mountains of Elbow Creek where now the sun was high and the light settled on them like

192

a softly shimmering mantle in the perfect silence.

'He had that sure enough—at a price,' he murmured.

'But he will be at peace now,' said Tentrees. 'You can see and hear that it is so.'

You could at that, reckoned Heggerty.

They were two days making the journey back to Bliss, two days in which Heggerty rode quietly and for the most part alone, reflecting on the events at the Drift and Elbow Creek, the deaths and the final fate of the gold. 'Might've known Logan would've done somethin' like that,' he had mused. 'That was his thinkin'. It wasn't the gold that mattered. Mebbe it never had. Reckon I can figure on that.'

A day passed before Heggerty approached Tranter where he sat with the last of his sidekicks in the glow of a supper fire under the watchful gaze of the Apaches.

'Tentrees says as how Miss Joni had contacted Territorial Marshal Dane out

Oversands way,' he said. 'Should be in Bliss by the time we get there. I'm handin' y'self and yuh men over t'him. Guess he'll know best what t' do. One thing I wanted to clear up—yuh knew at the start who shot and hanged Joe Pine.'

'I knew,' grunted Tranter. 'One of Stone's men. And I knew Logan was somewheres about. He always was, ever since the raid. Yuh in the clear, Heggerty.' He had lifted a slow stare to Heggerty's eyes. 'Lucky f' Logan he happened across yuh.'

'Mebbe,' Heggerty had replied, and turned away to join Shiner and Tentrees.

'Yuh ridin' on after Bliss?' asked the old man.

'West,' said Heggerty firmly.

'Any place in particular?'

'No place. As I find it.'

'Man can draw himself a heap of trouble just driftin'.' Shiner eyed him sharply. 'Yuh always been livin' by them guns, mister?'

'Survivin'. I never shot a man as didn't have his chance. The odds are always

194

even—'ceptin' that I don't wait t' blink!'

'That I'd figured!' grinned Shiner.

'Miss Joni would like you to stay at the homestead for a while,' said Tentrees. 'As long as you think fit. There is much to prepare for the future.'

'She'll manage fine,' said Heggerty. 'As long as yuh stay with her. But I'll be there t' say goodbye.'

It was another day before Heggerty, Tentrees and Shiner rode together along that same dusty trail from Bliss to the homestead on the edge of the desert. The sprawling miles of sand still shimmered in the high afternoon sun and the only shade lay across the home's veranda where Charlie Maggs's chair waited for his ghost to come and sit and watch and reflect on the far horizons.

TWENTY

'Yuh mind settled on leavin'?' asked Joni Maggs as she strolled with Heggerty round the homestead in the fresh morning air.

Heggerty turned to look at the girl again. He had watched her carefully in the half-hour they had spent relishing the cool of the early morning. There was a new bloom in her cheeks, a brighter, livelier gleam in her eyes; her yellow hair was tied back in the familiar tomboyish pony-tail he had first seen, and there was a sprightly, almost sensual energy in her young body. Whatever her ordeals at the hands of the Stone gang, she had put them aside, firmly into a past that would always have its shadows but maybe a fading substance.

Heggerty smiled. ''Fraid so. It's m' way,' he said quietly. 'Never known any other.'

The girl returned the smile. 'Guessed it first day I saw yuh. Yuh got the look.'

She linked her hands behind her back and scuffed a toecap through the dirt. 'Can't rightly blame yuh. Thought of doin' the same m'self on occasions. Never gotten t' it, and shan't now.' She halted and let her gaze take in the sprawl of the homestead. 'Reckon m' place is here. Charlie would've wanted that. There ain't a deal of money, but Tentrees and me figure we can work hard and build the spread up. And Shiner reckons his days of gold-diggin' are over. He'd like t' stay here, and he'd sure be welcome.' She walked on again. 'But that ain't what I really wanted t' say. I wanted t' say—'

'Don't,' said Heggerty sharply. 'There ain't no need f' a spoutin' of words.'

Joni halted again, turned her face to Heggerty and took his hand in hers. 'Yuh're the boss, mister! I ain't arguin' no more. But how about this...' She drew herself to him and kissed him, then rested her head on his shoulder. 'That say enough?'

'In full,' murmured Heggerty.

He slid an arm round her waist and they strolled on in silence.

Bliss was still bustling when Heggerty reined the mare to a canter on the outskirts facing the main street. 'Easy, gal. Easy,' he soothed as he slowed the mount to a walk.

He could have turned directly west after leaving the homestead, but for some reason he had no mind to figure, he had stayed on the main trail. Maybe he had been giving himself a good excuse to keep Joni, Tentrees and Shiner in his sights for as long as he could. Maybe he had wanted to make that one last wave and hold to the memory of theirs.

Or maybe he had wanted a final look at Bliss.

He passed the livery where the search for the gold shipment and the hunting down of the Stone gang had first come to life in that strange encounter with Marshal Josh Logan; the hotel where the marshal had unfolded his bitter story, and paused briefly at the blase, bustling saloon Crystal had used as her front for a far more treacherous haul of riches. He rode on again, passing the jail where Tranter had held him, and was about to urge the mare to a canter when Marshal Dane hailed him from the open door of the sheriff's office.

'Heggerty! Hey, Heggerty! Yuh hold it right there!'

Heggerty reined and waited.

'Yuh movin' out?' asked the marshal. 'Yeah, yuh movin' out. I see that plain as day.' The tall, broad-shouldered lawman came to the top of the steps that led to the office. 'I was just about t' ride out t' the Maggs place. Got some news f' yuh.'

Heggerty waited in silence.

'We been makin' arrangements t' move that gold from Cloud Drift. Bank here is keen t' get it under lock and key. Yuh fancy ridin' with us?'

'I reckon I'll give that a miss,' said Heggerty. 'But thanks f' the offer.'

'Suit y'self,' smiled Dane. 'Didn't somehow reckon the prospect would have much appeal anyhow. Meantime, the bank here reckons there's a fair reward due t' yuh f' what yuh did. Yuh goin' t' collect?'

Heggerty reflected for a moment. 'No, I guess not,' he said quietly. 'But I'd be grateful if yuh'd pass it on t' Miss Joni. She could use it well enough.'

'Yuh sure?' asked the marshal.

'I'm sure,' said Heggerty.

The marshal shrugged and scratched his head as he watched Heggerty ride on and turn to the open country heading West.

'Some men yuh can never figure,' he murmured to himself.

This Large Print Book for the Partially sighted, who cannot read normal print, is published under the auspices of

THE ULVERSCROFT FOUNDATION

THE ULVERSCROFT FOUNDATION

. . . we hope that you have enjoyed this Large Print Book. Please think for a moment about those people who have worse eyesight problems than you . . . and are unable to even read or enjoy Large Print, without great difficulty.

You can help them by sending a donation, large or small to:

**The Ulverscroft Foundation,
1, The Green, Bradgate Road,
Anstey, Leicestershire, LE7 7FU,
England.**

or request a copy of our brochure for more details.

The Foundation will use all your help to assist those people who are handicapped by various sight problems and need special attention.

Thank you very much for your help.

Other DALES Western Titles In Large Print

ELLIOT CONWAY
The Dude

JOHN KILGORE
Man From Cherokee Strip

J. T. EDSON
Buffalo Are Coming

ELLIOT LONG
Savage Land

HAL MORGAN
The Ghost Of Windy Ridge

NELSON NYE
Saddle Bow Slim

Other DALES Western Titles In Large Print

BILL WADE
Dead Come Sundown

JIM CLEVELAND
Colt Thunder

AMES KING
Death Rides The Thunderhead

NELSON NYE
The Marshal Of Pioche

RAY HOGAN
Gun Trap At Arabella

BEN BRIDGES
Mexico Breakout

THE CHAMELEON